Mousemagic

Animal Magic

Have you read them all?

1. Catmagic
2. Dogmagic
3. Hamstermagic
4. Rabbitmagic
5. Birdmagic
6. Ponymagic
7. Mousemagic

Look out for more books by
HOLLY WEBB

EMILY FEATHER
and the Enchanted Door

www.holly-webb.com

Animal Magic

Mouse Magic

HOLLY WEBB

Scholastic Children's Books
An imprint of Scholastic Ltd
Euston House, 24 Eversholt Street
London, NW1 1DB, UK
Registered office: Westfield Road, Southam, Warwickshire, CV47 0RA
SCHOLASTIC and associated logos are trademarks and/or
registered trademarks of Scholastic Inc.

First published in the UK by Scholastic Ltd, 2011
This edition published by Scholastic Ltd, 2013

Text copyright © Holly Webb, 2011

The right of Holly Webb to be identified as the author
of this work has been asserted by her.

ISBN 978 1 407 13558 8

A CIP catalogue record for this book is available
from the British Library.

Printed and bound by CPI Group (UK) Ltd, Croydon, CR0 4YY
Papers used by Scholastic Children's Books are made from
wood grown in sustainable forests.

3 5 7 9 10 8 6 4 2

This is a work of fiction. Names, characters, places, incidents
and dialogues are products of the author's imagination or are used
fictitiously. Any resemblance to actual people, living or dead,
events or locales is entirely coincidental.

www.scholastic.co.uk/zone

For Jon, Tom, Robin and William

Chapter 1

Lottie hurried through Netherbridge with Ruby. Sofie, Lottie's dog, waltzed around their feet, her long dachshund ears blowing in the cold November wind. The girls had been up on Netherbridge Hill, and they were late going home – Lottie's mum was cooking her a special birthday dinner, but Lottie was sure that she'd understand. She wished her mum could have been up on the hill with them, to see the herd of unicorns galloping past.

"Ugh, it's so dark!" Ruby moaned as they scuttled down the street to the pet shop. "Wintry."

Lottie shivered. "If it had been this cold last weekend, we wouldn't have needed to go to Linford for my skating party. We could have just skated on the river."

Just before they reached the shop, Ruby pulled Lottie's sleeve. "Listen, I just want to say thank you, Lottie. Seeing the unicorns like that, thundering down the hill. I think it was the best thing I've ever seen. They were so beautiful."

Lottie smiled, and gave Ruby a quick hug. "They're amazing, aren't they? I think that might be the best birthday present ever."

Lottie had woken that morning with the fleeting wisps of a dream, the horsey voice of Midnight, the black unicorn, laughing in her ear and telling her *Happy birthday*. She knew she had to go to Netherbridge Hill – it had been hard to live through a whole day at school first.

Now, she flung the door of the pet shop open, sighing delightedly as the warm, rather stuffy, slightly mouse-smelling air wafted round her. Lottie leant against the glass door, smiling.

Every so often, when she walked into the shop, she would get a sudden rush of astonishment that she really lived here. She was so lucky.

It was hardly surprising that she was happy. Lottie had adored Grace's Pet Shop when it only contained her uncle Jack and her cousin Danny. She had always loved animals, and living in a pet shop was like a dream come true, even if at first her uncle and Danny had been a bit weird and secretive.

It hadn't taken her that long to find out why. Grace's was no ordinary pet shop. All the animals could talk — in fact, several of them found it hard to stop. Uncle Jack had an amazing magic with animals, a magic that ran in the family, and wonderfully, Lottie had it too.

But now the shop seemed even more precious and special. Her father was there, for a start, looking just like a more tanned version of Uncle Jack. Even more brilliantly, Lottie's mother was in the kitchen, making Lottie's favourite tea, shepherd's pie. To most people, that wouldn't sound all that strange, Lottie thought to herself – except that for years everyone had thought her dad was dead. And until just a few weeks before, her mum had been living and working in Paris. It was why Lottie had been dumped at the shop back at the beginning of the summer – that was how she'd thought of it then. Now it was the best thing that had ever happened to her.

Her mum was mashing potatoes and humming to herself, but she glanced up as Lottie and Ruby came into the kitchen, and the look on her face made Lottie feel like singing – loudly. There was a smear of mashed potato down her mum's cheek and her hair was falling out of its ponytail, and she was beaming. Lottie had never seen her look prettier. Her dad was sitting at the table, pretending to look at a catalogue for a pet food company, but actually watching her mum. They weren't back together as a couple – they had been apart for so long, eight whole years, and were still getting to know each other again – but Lottie was hoping.

"Did you see them?" Lottie's mum asked, rubbing absent-mindedly at the potato streak, her eyes searching Lottie's face eagerly.

Lottie nodded slowly. She felt almost as though she were dreaming. Her mother, her own mother, the person who couldn't stand animals, and laughed at anything even slightly mysterious, let alone magical, was asking if she'd seen a herd of unicorns.

The unicorns came from a lost forest in the foothills of the Himalayas. Her dad had lived with them, trapped without his memory, for all that time he had been missing. He had almost been transformed into a unicorn, and only Lottie's growing magic had brought him home, the magic fizzing in her blood calling to his. Lottie had thought the strange encounters she had with a silver unicorn were only dreams. She hadn't known she'd was gradually breaking the spell that had been put on her own father.

It was the kind of story her sensible mother would never have believed. Lottie hadn't known it, but her mum's disbelieving attitude to magic had been partly down to her dad's old girlfriend. Pandora had never got over breaking up with Lottie's dad. She had been crazily, murderously jealous, and she'd been the one who sent Lottie's dad off to get lost in the unicorns' forest. She'd also poisoned Lottie's mum's mind to magic. But Pandora was gone now – banished to the rainforest herself.

A pair of soft grey ears appeared over the edge of the table, and then, slowly, a greyish-pink nose and a pair of dark, solemn eyes. Barney the rabbit had come to investigate what his favourite person was doing.

"Hello, Barney darling," Lottie's mum stroked the back of her arm across his ears. Barney had helped to turn her back into an animal person, and she adored him, but she would never have dreamed of stroking an

6

animal with her hand while she was in the middle of cooking. Lottie sort of understood this, and she could see why it was a good idea, but she and Uncle Jack still caught each other's eye. Uncle Jack usually cooked with an owl on one shoulder and quite possibly a mouse or two in his hair. The owl, Horace, was actually a phoenix in disguise, but Lottie was pretty sure phoenixes weren't particularly hygienic either.

"More butter, if you please." Sofie popped up on the other side of the table and stared critically at the pan of mashed potato. "It looks dry to me."

Lottie's mum raised one eyebrow, but then she shrugged, and stirred the potato thoughtfully. "Perhaps a little," she conceded.

Sofie nodded as she stirred it in, and sniffed the buttery steam with her eyes closed. "*Magnifique*." Then she snapped her eyes open again and glared at Lottie's mum. "Of course, it is not French cuisine," she pointed out sternly.

"Of course not." Lottie's mum passed a spoonful of potato quite close to Sofie's nose. "Does that mean you don't want any?"

"When in Rome. . ." Sofie said in a long-suffering voice. "I am not one to complain. Ever."

"It smells fantastic," Lottie murmured, giving her mum a quick one-arm hug so as not to get in the way of the dinner. "Will it be long? It was freezing out on the hill and I'm so hungry."

"Me too," Ruby added. "It looks great."

"Did they look all right, the unicorns?" Lottie's dad asked, rather wistfully. "Was it the whole herd?"

"I think so." Lottie half-closed her eyes, remembering and trying to count. "Definitely fifty at least. They came galloping across the ridge. It was amazing. Ruby nearly fell over, it was so exciting."

"I've never seen anything like that." Ruby

sat down at the table, her chin in her hands, smiling.

"There." Lottie's mum finished spooning the mash over the pie, and slid it into the oven. "That should be ready before we know it."

"Where's Danny?" Lottie asked. "Is he upstairs?"

Uncle Jack nodded. "In his room."

"Are you two planning on changing for this special birthday dinner?" Lottie's mum asked, her voice very bright. Lottie took the hint. Uncle Jack was looking gloomy enough as it was. It looked like Danny had done something wrong. Probably he'd been rude to Lottie's mum again; he seemed to be doing that a lot at the moment.

Ever since she and Lottie's dad had both been back at the shop, Danny had been very moody. Lottie hated it. Danny's mum had died a few years ago, and it had been something that tied him and Lottie together – only having one parent. Now Lottie had a whole perfect family, and Danny was furiously, meanly jealous.

Ruby had brought some things to change into, so they headed upstairs, Sofie galloping in front of them. She had a selection of glittery collars, and clearly she wanted to dress up too.

"This is great, having a special family party," Ruby told Lottie.

Lottie grinned. "I know. Mum and me always had a special meal on my birthday, but it was just the two of us. This year it's huge. And I've already had my proper party with you and people from school last weekend." She ran a brush through her black curly hair, tugging it thoughtfully. "I feel spoilt."

Sofie pushed in front of Ruby to see herself in the mirror. "Hmm. The purple crystals, I think. Lottie, fasten me." She held out her long neck gracefully. "*Merci, ma petite*. Are we ready?" She gazed round at Ruby and Lottie, rather like a bossy little headmistress, and trotted out of the room, with the girls trooping after her.

Uncle Jack was at the bottom of the stairs, having words with Danny. ". . .Lottie's birthday! Just behave yourself!" He shut up quickly when he heard Sofie's claws clattering on the wooden treads, and shooed Danny into the kitchen.

"Still causing trouble, then?" Ruby whispered. She usually got on well with Danny – they'd been at the same school until this year, when he'd gone off to secondary school.

"All the time," Lottie muttered. "But I can see why, I guess." She sighed. She hoped Danny got used to the way things were soon. She didn't think she could bear it if her mum or dad ended up leaving again.

"She's coming, she's coming!" A whisper ran round the cages in the shop as Lottie and Ruby reached the bottom of the stairs. A moving, mottled carpet of mice rushed in front of them to reach the kitchen first, and a chorus of different voices called, "Happy birthday, Lottie!"

The mice were lined up all along the shelves of the dresser, dancing and squeaking with excitement. Lottie's favourite pink mouse, Fred, had made himself a matching pink party hat, a dashing, pointed creation, which threatened to fall off every time he moved.

"He looks ridiculous," Sofie muttered. She found Fred deeply irritating, and would not admit that it was because she was jealous. She was Lottie's familiar, her special one, but she could never quite believe that Lottie loved her best.

Lottie looked round the kitchen hopefully, wondering where her presents were. She had agreed to have them after tea, so that there wasn't a rush before school, but now the waiting was starting to get to her.

They must be all hidden away somewhere, the cake too, Lottie thought. At least, she hoped so. Maybe everyone thought eleven was too old for proper presents.

But the table looked beautiful, with loads of tiny candles glittering all over it, and all her family packed around. It was a squash to fit everyone in. Ariadne – Uncle Jack's girlfriend, who taught Lottie magic – had arrived and was sitting next to Uncle Jack. Tabitha, her cat familiar, was balanced on her shoulder, blinking slowly at the mice, who were trying very hard to ignore her. They *knew* that Tabitha would never chase them here, but their instincts were still telling them that she wanted *them* for dinner, not shepherd's pie.

"Is it time for presents yet?" Fred asked hopefully, as soon as Lottie had taken a bite of pie. "You said when you'd eaten!" he complained, as Uncle Jack shook his head. "Honestly, I do wish you'd all hurry up."

Lottie smiled in secret relief. So there were going to be presents. She'd known it really, but just for a moment. . . She felt almost as impatient as Fred.

"Now?" Fred squeaked. He'd skittered up

the tablecloth as Lottie's mum was clearing the plates, and was now sitting next to a small tea light holder by Lottie, warming his paws and exchanging dirty looks with Sofie.

"Cake first." Uncle Jack got up to turn the lights off, so that only the candles lit the room. Hundreds of tiny, eager eyes glittered in the flickering light.

"Oh. . ." Lottie breathed, as her mother walked in from the shop – where on earth had they hidden the cake so that no one nibbled it? She smiled to herself. Perhaps they'd set Horace to guard it. In his owl shape, he was most of the mice's worst nightmare.

It was huge. Pink and white icing, with eleven tall pink candles. Lottie's mum had always made fabulous birthday cakes, but this one was so grown-up.

"Happy birthday dear Lottie, happy birthday to you. . . !" Growls and squeaks joined together, and everyone finished at a different time, but Lottie didn't mind. The happiness rippled in the air. The mice, especially, seemed to be in a state of nervous excitement that made Lottie's heart race like theirs were. There was a secret, something terribly exciting. She could feel it inside her.

Lottie's dad had put an armful of parcels in front of her while her mum was cutting up the cake, and now he grinned at her. "I'd hurry up, before Fred has a heart attack."

"I am perfectly all right, thank you!" Fred declared, standing up and sticking out his chest. But then he spoilt the effect by twisting his tail between his tiny paws, and adding, "But do please hurry, Lottie! We want to give you our present!" Then he sat down very quickly, with a nervous giggle.

Lottie stared at the presents, wondering which to open first. In the end she closed her eyes, and reached. A small silver-wrapped parcel. No ribbon. From her dad. She smiled at him, and undid the tape. Inside was a little velvet bag, and Lottie opened it curiously. Into her hand fell a delicate coil of silver chain, with a silver unicorn dangling from it. The pendant was only tiny, but as Lottie stared at it, she could see every hair. She could feel its heart beating under her fingers, and if she closed her eyes, she could smell the rich, earthy steam of the rainforest.

"Midnight's hair is inside it," her father explained. "The one we used to get back to the rainforest. I thought you'd like it – I don't know if we'll ever go back. . ."

"I love it. Thank you. . ." She hugged him, and he fastened it carefully round her neck.

"Go on! Go on!" Fred was dancing about again.

Lottie's mum had given her a bracelet that matched the unicorn necklace (which was good, Lottie noted at the back of her mind, as it meant that her mum and dad had talked about presents together). Ruby's present was a cool velvet scarf, purple with silvery stripes. Uncle Jack had given her a book on scorpions, which Lottie rather thought he'd wanted for himself, and Ariadne's present was a big, purple-covered book, embossed on the front cover with SPELLS. But it turned out to be empty.

"You have to write the spells in, Lottie, when you make them up," Ariadne told her, chuckling at her confused face. "That will be the next stage of your training – refining and perfecting your spells, and writing them down."

Sofie nudged a small package towards her. She was pretending not to care what Lottie thought, gulping at her cake as Lottie undid it, but she was glaring sharply sideways. It had no tape or ribbon, which made Lottie think that Sofie had wrapped it herself, which must have been almost impossible with paws. "Oh, Sofie," she murmured, as she pulled it out. A tiny gold-framed painting of a dachshund. It wasn't quite Sofie – the nose was longer – but it was very like her.

"My grandmother." Sofie ducked her nose

proudly as Lottie kissed her head. "It is old. Take care, yes?"

"Of course I will."

Danny made a dismissive sort of snorting noise, and Lottie looked up in surprise. Sofie leaned further forward over the table, and hissed, "You have something to say, Daniel, huh?"

"Do you have a present for Lottie, Danny?" Uncle Jack asked hurriedly, trying to smooth things over.

"No," Danny snapped. "What else does she need? She's got everything, hasn't she?" He scraped his chair back with a nerve-jarring screech, grabbed Septimus, his black rat, and ran off upstairs, banging the kitchen door behind him.

Everyone sat staring at each other dumbly, until Fred squeaked. "More presents!"

"Yes, yes! Now us, now us!" The mice chittered and giggled, and Fred scurried off the table to be surrounded by a crowd of

18

overexcited mice on the front of the dresser.

"Hurry up!" Lottie could hear him hissing. "No, not that tight, I'll faint! There!" and the mice drew back, letting Fred stand in front of them all, blushing a darker pink than usual.

He was wearing a large purple satin ribbon tied in a bow around his middle, and his whiskers were drooping with bashfulness.

"This is our present," he gabbled. "Me."

Chapter 2

"Hmf!" Sofie snorted disgustedly. "That is ridiculous!"

The mice erupted in squeaky indignation.

"It's not!"

"How dare she?"

"What can you expect from a dog?"

Lottie reached out her hand, and Fred stepped into it. She could feel that he was trembling, his whole tiny body shivering in her fingers. "You look beautiful," she told him, stroking his head with the tip of one finger. She wanted to tell Fred how much she loved him, and how happy it made her that he wanted to belong to her. But she could feel Sofie in her mind, seething.

He's just a mouse, Sofie. . .

Exactly!

He doesn't want to be my familiar. Only you can be that. And you know I wouldn't let him, anyway. It's sweet.

It is sneaky.

But I can't tell him no!

Lottie felt Sofie's soft, velvety brown voice curl away from her, tucking back inside the dog. There was a cold little whisper instead. *I suppose not.*

Lottie glanced back. Sofie was still sitting up at the table, but she'd stopped nibbling the icing off her slice of birthday cake. Now she had her chin resting on her little auburn paws, and she was staring dolefully at the sugar roses. Lottie bit her lip. She knew how jealous Sofie could be. She had actually run away once, after she thought Lottie preferred Barney the rabbit to her, which of course Lottie didn't.

Please don't be angry with me!

Sofie's ears flickered, but she didn't look up.

Sofie, you know I love you best!

Sofie's tail twitched, and she darted Lottie a little sideways glance. *More than that little pink thing? You like pink.*

I like Fred. He's a friend. But he's not you, and... and you know that. You're just trying to make me say it, aren't you? That you're the special one. Sofie, that's mean!

Sofie chuckled into her paws. *I was making sure, that is all. Tell the little pink thing that purple doesn't suit him, Lottie. And remember you are MINE.*

Lottie felt Fred's whiskers tickling her fingers. He was gazing up at her, his black-button eyes snapping with crossness. "Sorry," she told him quickly. "I was just. . ."

"That dog has you wrapped round her paws, Lottie," Fred told her sternly. "You were asking her permission. Don't try to deny it."

"Be grateful that Lottie's familiar is not a cat." Tabitha had jumped silently from Ariadne's shoulder, and picked her way down the table, her delicate tabby paws padding

22

carefully around the tea lights. "*I* would not allow a mouse anywhere near Ariadne."

"Cats are terribly jealous. It is well known." Sofie was sitting up straight again now, her dark eyes gleaming at the thought of a spat with Tabitha. They respectfully disliked each other.

"Stop it. No more fighting on my birthday," Lottie said, letting Fred climb into a fold of the purple striped scarf that Ruby had given her. She could feel him glowing with satisfaction next to her ear. From the disgusted expression lurking around Tabitha's whiskers, she suspected that Fred had stuck his tongue out at the cat.

"Have you had a good birthday?" Lottie's mum asked, as she said goodnight to her later. She was sitting on the end of Lottie's bed, and Lottie was leaning against her pillows, stroking the silver unicorn necklace.

"Brilliant." Lottie smiled at her. "It's the

first one I can remember with you and Dad both here."

Her mum nodded. "It felt special for me too." She was silent for a moment, and then she added, "I've got one more present for you."

Lottie sat up excitedly. She couldn't see any parcels.

Her mum grinned. "You can't unwrap it; sorry, sweetheart. It's that I've decided we should definitely stay in Netherbridge."

"You have? But what about your job? You said you weren't sure you could find a job here."

Lottie's mum nodded. "I know, and I haven't, so far. But since that strange day when we went to the rainforest, somehow I feel as though I understand more about the magic in you. I can't take you away from all this, especially now you have your dad here. And I don't want to have to leave you and go back to my old job. I hated being away from you when I was in France."

Lottie wondered hopefully if her mum didn't want to go away and leave her dad as well. It had been really hard so far, stopping herself from asking them whether they were going to get back together. She was desperate to know, and at the same time, she didn't want to push it, in case they said no, they'd been apart for too long, or something awful like that.

"So, where will we live?" she whispered. And Sofie wriggled down to Lottie's mum's end of the bed, and laid her heavy little muzzle on Lottie's mum's lap.

"Can we live here?" Sofie murmured.

"I mentioned it to your uncle Jack, and he didn't seem to mind." Lottie's mum traced the pattern on her skirt with one finger. "It's not ideal, of course, your dad sleeping on the floor in that little office. . ."

Her mum trailed off, staring vaguely at the pink wallpaper, and Lottie watched her hopefully. But all her mum did was shake her head briskly and smile. "You'd better get some sleep, Lottie! It's late, and you've got school tomorrow."

Lottie nodded, and curled up under her duvet, with Sofie under one arm, and Fred wriggled into a small nest he'd made for himself out of an old sock, which he'd tucked into the crevice between Lottie's pillow and the side of the bed.

All in all, it had been a very good birthday. . .

When Lottie came down for breakfast the next morning, it was clear that Danny's mood from the previous night hadn't improved.

"I don't see why not," Danny was snarling across the breakfast table, and Lottie's mum eyed him, half surprised, half nervous.

Lottie caught the scene from the kitchen door – she'd come downstairs ten minutes later than Danny, because he'd deliberately run ahead of her and nicked the bathroom, just when she'd been going for a shower. She shook her head, knowing that if she'd spoken to Mum like that she'd have lost about a month's pocket money.

"I just don't think birthday cake is a very sensible breakfast," her mum said gently. "What about toast?"

"I hate toast."

Lottie caught her mother's eye, and grinned. They'd both seen Danny demolishing huge towers of toast, cemented together with layers of peanut butter. Toast was what he ate whenever he felt even slightly hungry – which was all the time.

"Don't laugh at me!" Danny snapped, and Lottie immediately felt guilty. She hated it when people gave her that kind of amused look; it made her feel like a two-year-old having a tantrum. And she could hear how miserable Danny was under all the stroppiness.

"If he was a mouse, I'd just thump him with a bag of sunflower seeds," Fred whispered. He was lurking behind Lottie's orange juice now, and he mimed whacking Danny over the head. Lottie nodded while Danny was safely glaring at her mum. It was tempting.

"Well, what about cornflakes?" her mum was suggesting now, looking hopefully at the kitchen door, obviously wishing Uncle Jack would arrive. She pushed the cornflakes packet towards Danny, but he didn't take it. He simply went on glaring.

Lottie shivered. She could feel the air in the kitchen turning into something that felt like cold treacle, full of fury. Was it Danny's magic? Danny hardly ever used his powers. Lottie often wondered whether his magic was stronger, because he left it sitting around, bubbling away inside him. Or did magic get better with practice, like playing the violin? She wasn't sure. She felt a gentle nudge against her leg, and looked down to see Sofie, her dark eyes round and worried. She scrambled up on to Lottie's lap, but didn't demand an immediate cup of coffee. Instead she and Lottie stared at

Danny's face, horribly white under his black curls. Septimus was standing on the table in front of him, his tail swishing and coiling like a snake. It looked as though he was having a silent argument – or trying to. Lottie got the feeling Danny wasn't listening.

Her mum didn't seem to notice the atmosphere. "Shall I pour you some?"

Lottie winced. Poor Mum, she was trying so hard. She waited for Danny to yell at her.

But he didn't. He curved his lips in an unconvincing smile. "Yeah." He even added, "Please."

Lottie drew in a breath, suddenly certain that something was wrong. What was he doing? "Mum. . ."

Her mother glanced across, her expression so relieved at avoiding an argument. "Do you want some too, Lottie?" Then she looked back down at the cereal packet, unfolding the cardboard flaps.

The treacly air seemed to shatter into glassy

splinters as she screamed.

Lottie jumped up, and only the comfort of Sofie in her arms stopped her joining in. Perched on the plastic liner of the cereal box, legs fumbling in a confused sort of way, as though it had suddenly found itself somewhere unexpected, was the largest spider Lottie had ever seen.

Her mum was frozen, one hand still stretched out towards the packet, the other clamped across her mouth, probably to stop her being sick.

Lottie hated spiders. She didn't squash them, but she tended to leave the room fast when one turned up. But her mum was much, much worse.

"I'll . . . I'll move it, Mum, don't worry," she muttered, her voice sounding strangely squeaky.

"They *eat* mice." Fred was peeking around the juice glass, and Lottie was sure he'd gone a shade paler. "I'm breakfast. . . Oh. . ." And he flopped backwards very artistically, making sure to arrange his tail nicely as he fainted on to a napkin.

There was a thudding sound as someone raced down the wooden stairs, and Lottie's dad appeared in the kitchen, with Horace gliding behind him.

"Isobel! What is it?" He grabbed Lottie's mum and dragged her away from the table, and even the spider, still waving its legs around the cereal box, couldn't stop the jolt of excitement Lottie felt at seeing her mum hug him back.

"A spider! Huge. . ."

Lottie's dad speared Danny with a look, but Danny only smirked and poured himself a glass of juice.

Lottie caught her breath as her dad nodded at Horace. He might only be a pygmy owl at the moment, but Horace adored spiders, the bigger the better. He swooped low over the table, snatched up the horrid leggy thing in his claws, and flapping hard to carry the extra weight, he disappeared discreetly to eat his luxury breakfast in the shop.

Uncle Jack ducked to avoid the legs trailing in his hair as he came in. "What was that Horace had?" he demanded. "I didn't order any tarantulas, did I?" Uncle Jack was a bit overenthusiastic about stock sometimes, and occasionally there were unexpected deliveries. "I hope it wasn't expensive," he muttered, as a particularly disgusting squelchy crunch echoed out from the shop. "And I bet you anything he's eating it in the front window. Horace! Don't do that! There might be customers passing!"

"Where did you get it from, mmm?" Sofie leaned across the table to stare at Danny.

Danny just shrugged. "Found it."

"That was *you*?" Lottie's mum sounded so hurt, even Danny looked ashamed of himself for a second.

Sofie frowned at her, the furry skin between

her eyes wrinkling. "Did you think it just appeared in the cornflakes by accident?"

"I was going to complain," Lottie's mum said weakly. "To the manufacturer. . ." Then she shook herself, biting hard on her bottom lip. "What did I do?" she asked Danny, so quietly that everyone had to strain to hear.

Danny said nothing for a few seconds, and then he stared up at her coldly. "How about coming back to play happy families with Lottie and Uncle Tom? Well, sorry, not everyone's happy."

Uncle Jack went bright red at that, and grounded Danny, for ever apparently. He scooped Septimus off the kitchen table and scowled down at the black rat.

"Why didn't you stop him?"

Septimus attempted to shrug, but it didn't work very well. "I couldn't," he muttered. Lottie had never heard him sound less relaxed. He was normally a very laid-back rat.

Uncle Jack ran one finger along the ends of

Sep's whiskers, which left him shaking his head dazedly – and then he flopped on to the table with his paws in the air.

"What did you do to him?" Danny yelled, jumping up and trying to grab his rat back.

"He's confined to the shop. Just like you," his father told him shortly, passing him a handful of dopey rat. "Perhaps grounding you will actually mean something now. Don't worry, he'll be back to his usual rude self in a few minutes. But he won't be going with you to school – not until you get your act together and start behaving like a member of this family again."

"This is so unfair," Danny growled, but Lottie noticed he was cradling Septimus close to his school sweater, stroking him lovingly. She was suddenly glad that Danny had Sep, when he was so upset and angry with everyone else.

Lottie's mum was still leaning against her dad, her face pale. Spiders really made her feel ill – Lottie had hugged her after she'd been frightened by one, and knew that her heart would be hammering against her father's arms.

"Sit down." Lottie's dad nudged her into a chair. "I'll make you some tea."

She nodded, staring down at the table, her cheeks pink with embarrassment. "I'm sorry." She glanced over at Uncle Jack. "I know it's stupid to be so scared of them."

Uncle Jack shook his head. "You've seen me at picnics, Isobel. It's wasps for me. Everyone has something silly like that. Not everyone has a nephew who deliberately upsets them, though," he added.

Danny huddled silently in his chair now, waiting anxiously for Sep to wake up from the spell. Lottie watched him, seeing how miserable he looked. She wanted to be angry – that would be easier. But she couldn't help feeling desperately sorry for him.

Chapter 3

"I can't believe you're being so nice about it!" Ruby's blue eyes were as round as marbles. "*And* I can't believe he would do something that horrible! I mean, even I would have screamed, and I don't mind spiders or crawly things that much. Which is lucky, actually, seeing as live crickets are Sam and Joe's favourite food."

Sam and Joe were Ruby's pet lizards. They claimed that they were actually dragons, but they were short on the flying and the breathing fire. Lottie wasn't sure whether to believe them or not, but Sam and Joe certainly seemed to believe it themselves. They hadn't told Ruby yet – she just thought they were rare and exotic. Ruby didn't have strong magic like Lottie, but she could hear animals talk. Sam and Joe had been able to tell that she was special, and they had persuaded her into buying them from an enormous pet shop, where they had ended up by accident. Ruby and her mother had gone into the shop to buy a hamster. It had been a bit of a shock when they got home and realized that somehow they'd bought two huge pale-blue lizards, and rather a lot of expensive lizard equipment.

Lottie smiled, huddling into the corner of the bench. It was freezing, but all the teachers were convinced that fresh air was important at break, and so they had to go out. "Well, his plan totally didn't work," she explained. "Usually, I wouldn't have spoken to him for ages, but you should have seen it, Ruby." She rubbed her hands together for warmth. "Mum and Dad. Dad came in, you see, and hugged her, and sent Horace after the spider. It was like he was a prince, and he'd rescued her and slain a dragon. And when I left for school, they were still sitting drinking tea and chatting, like I've never seen." She closed her eyes like a sunbathing cat, contented and hopeful. "I'm just so glad they're getting along."

Lottie smiled to herself, remembering her skating birthday party at the weekend. Her parents had skated too, and it was obviously something they'd done together before. They'd looked amazing – hand in hand, skimming happily around the crowds of slower skaters, their feet moving in rhythm. "At my birthday party, they looked, well. . ."

She sighed out a wistful breath. She only hoped they had seen it too – how well they fitted together, even now, after eight years apart.

"Are you thinking about when they were skating together? They did look happy," Ruby said quietly, as though she wasn't sure if this was something she was allowed to comment on.

Lottie gave her a swift, embarrassed grin, feeling silly to be caught so obviously building dream worlds.

Then she shrugged. "I say I'm only hoping they can be friends, but I'm not even convincing me," she sighed. "Really I want them to get back together, but I just don't want to push my luck."

"If Danny sets any more horrible traps, I'm never coming to sleep over again," Ruby warned.

Lottie giggled. "I don't think he'd dare. I'd never seen Uncle Jack so angry, except with Pandora. Danny looked pretty surprised about it too. I think Uncle Jack lets him get away with stuff mostly. It's just easier that way. But this time he was furious."

Ruby nodded. "Good!"

"Hey, Lottie! Look at the massive bruise I got from Saturday!" A girl with a long blonde ponytail flumped down on the arm of the bench next to Lottie, and stretched out her leg to show off a startling greenish bruise.

"Ow!" Lottie said sympathetically. "Tyra, that looks really sore!"

"Skating was brilliant, though, wasn't it?" Another girl, this one with short brown curly hair, squeezed on to the bench next to Ruby.

Lottie nodded. "I loved it. I'm really glad you had a good time. And thanks for the pens, Sinead, they're brilliant, especially the glittery ones."

Tyra and Sinead were two girls in Lottie's class. Until quite recently she'd hardly spoken to them – and no one except Ruby dared to speak to *her*. Not because Lottie was scary, but because she was off limits, according to the queen of their class, Zara Martin. Zara had hated Lottie since the first time they met, just after Lottie had moved to Netherbridge. She had the whole class, or at least the girls, so terrified that if she said no one was to speak to Lottie Grace, Lottie got left alone. Luckily, Ruby had been warring with Zara ever since they were both in Reception, and she'd been delighted to find a friend who seemed to see through Zara in the same way she did.

Recently Zara's hold over the school seemed to have died away a little. Now, when Zara was being her usual mean self, some people actually dared to answer her back. And everyone else in the class would look at her, or whisper behind her back, even if they didn't blame her outright. In other words, she was becoming just a little bit more like a normal person – except a very scary one.

It meant that Lottie felt far more part of things at school than she ever had done.

"Oh look! It's the weirdos." Somebody sniggered behind them, and Lottie and Ruby exchanged a weary glance.

Zara.

Of course, they should have expected it. She was bound to be furious that Lottie had dared to have a birthday party, and had invited Tyra and Sinead and her other friends, Lily and Emily. The four girls weren't particular friends of Zara's, but she regarded all the girls in the class as her property.

"So, did you enjoy your little *party*, Lottie?" Zara cooed, leaning over the back of the bench between them. Lottie could smell Zara's long brown hair, as it wafted close to her. It smelled of some horrible, sickly-sweet, flowery shampoo, and it made Lottie gag.

"It was brilliant, thanks," Ruby said coolly. She was still better at fighting back at Zara than Lottie was. She'd already had six years of practice.

"Yes." Lottie nodded, trying to slow down the anxious thump of her heart. She could tell that Zara was itching for a fight. The anger was buzzing all around her.

Lottie saw Lily and Emily lurking close by. They looked miserable and apologetic, and Lottie guessed that Zara had pumped them for information about the party. She smiled quickly at them, in a *don't worry* way, putting as much reassurance into the smile as she could. Lily and Emily smiled back, the frightened look leaving their faces, and then – Lottie hadn't expected this – they came closer, standing by the bench next to Lottie and smiling sweetly at Zara. Tyra and Sinead didn't make an excuse to disappear either, although Lottie could tell that Tyra was worried – she kept smoothing her skirt over her knees.

"Hi, Zara!" Emily gulped.

Bethany and the rest of Zara's little gang seemed to appear from nowhere, and Bethany even sat on the other arm of the bench, almost touching Ruby.

I've got my group, and she's got hers. It thudded through Lottie's thoughts. *We're equally matched.*

Of course it is not! Sofie snapped in her head, her voice sharp with crossness. *For a start you have me. And you are a witch, Lottie!*

A scared witch, Lottie pointed out.

You have already used one spell without even

43

thinking, Sofie told her. *That smile was perfect. Full of love, and need. Lily and Emily and the others are standing beside you, do you not see? Standing up to Zara? Have they ever done that before? I think not! Stop worrying that you need to do something clever. You have done it already! Zara sees! Look at her!*

Lottie turned to look up at Zara, and realized that Sofie was right. She had done something brave without even thinking about it. Zara was strangely blank-faced, and Lottie could tell that it was because behind that smooth mask, her mind was whirring away in a confused jumble.

But being Zara, that meant she was about to attack, her way. Lottie pasted a calm, I-don't-care smile on her face, and glanced at Ruby, who was wearing an identical smile.

Do not let her hurt you! Sofie whispered, sending images of herself as a furry scarf wrapping round Lottie.

I won't, Lottie promised. But her voice

sounded brittle, even to her, and she sat up very straight, as though it would help her to withstand Zara.

Zara leant her arms on the back of the bench and rested her chin on them, so she could flick her eyes between Lottie and Ruby.

"So, when are you moving in?" she asked Ruby.

Ruby blinked. "What?"

"To the pet shop. Everyone else Lottie knows seems to live there now. So I was just wondering when you were going to move."

"My family live at the shop, that's all," Lottie said calmly, rolling her eyes slightly at Ruby.

"I don't know how you fit everyone in." Zara smirked. "That shop isn't big enough to swing a cat, let alone house a family the size of yours."

"You would know about swinging cats," Lottie said sweetly. "Seeing as you make a habit of torturing them."

Only the second time Lottie had met Zara,

she and Sofie had had to rescue a stray cat from her and her mates. That poor, scraggly stray was actually Tabitha, who was now Ariadne's beautiful familiar, but Lottie still hadn't forgiven Zara for the way she'd treated the poor creature.

Zara flushed an angry red across her cheekbones, spoiling her pretty pink-and-white complexion. "Rubbish," she snapped.

Lottie shrugged. "I was there." She looked round at Bethany and Ellie and Amy. "So were you. What would you call it?"

Zara's clique were silent, embarrassed, and waiting for Zara to say something that would annihilate Lottie and stop her making them feel guilty.

Zara hissed in a breath through her teeth. She ignored Lottie's accusation about Tabitha and doubled back. "So now that your mum's back from France and your dad's turned up out of nowhere, when are you leaving?"

"She isn't," Ruby snapped.

"She was only supposed to be living with her uncle while her mum was in France, *I* thought," Zara purred with satisfaction. She could tell she'd upset Ruby.

"Well, now I'm staying." Lottie grinned. "Aren't you pleased, Zara?" She leant back against the bench and stared, smiling, right into Zara's china-blue eyes. It was something she'd never dared to do before, and at this close range, it felt like a declaration of war.

Emily and Lily sniggered, and Zara stood up, whirling her scented hair around her. "I really couldn't care less," she snarled. And she stalked off, Amy and Ellie and Bethany running after her like sheep.

Sinead gave a dismissive snort. "She's such an idiot!" she announced, but she sounded relieved that Zara had gone.

"Forget her!" Tyra waved Zara and her gang away. "Did you see, this morning? Mrs Laurence had the letters about Broom Manor!"

"Don't look so excited, Tyra. It's going to

47

be freezing." Lily shuddered. "Why can't we do it in the summer term, that's what I want to know."

"Costs the school more," Sinead told her.

Lottie blinked. She'd missed something here.

"Your sister went last year, didn't she, Lily?" Emily asked. "Did she have a good time?"

"She said it was brilliant. Muddy, though. Mum said her clothes nearly killed the washing machine. And Robbie Sinclair lost one of his wellies – it just got sucked under."

"Ugh." Emily made a face. "There's loads of indoor stuff, though, isn't there? A climbing wall?"

Tyra nodded. "And a pool."

Ruby nudged Lottie. "You probably haven't even heard about it! The trip?"

Lottie shook her head.

"It's a Year Six thing. Every year, at the end of the autumn term, we get to go away – for a whole week!" Ruby beamed at her.

"To this place in Yorkshire called Broom

Manor. It's an activity centre. Climbing, abseiling – all that team-building stuff." Emily waved a hand vaguely.

"I'm just glad Zara's not quite so bad any more," Lily frowned. "She isn't as scary somehow. Can you imagine being stuck with her night and day, though?"

Ruby shivered. "Perhaps we could infect her with chicken pox or something, so she can't go."

Lottie shook her head. "She's never ill, haven't you noticed? I should think the germs are too scared."

The others giggled, but the smile on Lottie's face suddenly froze. There was a strange worried silence in that corner at the back of her mind. The warm corner where she could usually feel Sofie snoozing on her velvet cushion. It took her a moment to realize what was wrong, and then she got it.

She finally understood what the school activity week was going to mean – a whole week away from all the animals in the shop, and most importantly, from Sofie.

Chapter 4

"You did not know?" Sofie sat watching her, head held to one side, bright eyes examining Lottie's face.

"NO!" Lottie stared at her. "Of course I didn't! I didn't even know this holiday happened!"

Sofie had met her at the door of the shop, sensing that she was coming. She had scrambled up into Lottie's arms, and Lottie had run upstairs with her, feeling Sofie's little heart beating like a butterfly's wings against her own.

"What are we going to do?" Lottie wailed, and slumped down on her bed.

Sofie wriggled up the bed to lay her nose on the pillow, just touching Lottie's ear. "I do not want to talk about it," she murmured sadly.

A small flash of pink appeared under Lottie's bedroom door, and Fred stood next to Lottie's bed, staring up at them indignantly.

"Well, thank you, Lottie, for saying hello to me so nicely as you raced past! Really, your manners are. . ." He trailed off, and scurried up the carved bed frame, so that he was looking down on Lottie and Sofie. "What's the matter? Did something go wrong at school?"

"No," Lottie sighed. "Well, sort of. I have to go on this school trip thing, and Sofie won't be able to come." She frowned. "Actually, do I have to go? What if we told the school we couldn't afford it? I know they pay some, but Mum will have to pay quite a lot of it. I don't think it's really that expensive, but I could tell Mrs Laurence the shop's not doing very well."

"You will not!" Sofie snapped, her whiskers vibrating with indignation. "What would that little beast Zara say if you went announcing all over the school that we had no money, hmm?"

Lottie made a *hmf* sort of noise. "I wouldn't care. But then Ruby would be standing up to Zara all on her own for a week. It wouldn't be fair. I have to go. Oh, how are we going to bear it, Sofie?"

Sofie snapped her teeth together. "More to the point, how are you going to manage without me? I am your – your common sense! Without me you will do all sorts of stupid things."

"I have common sense!" Lottie said rather indignantly. "You're my chocolate-obsessed side, that's all." She hugged Sofie. "I don't mean it. You make me brave, Sofie, ever so much more than I am on my own." She shuddered. On her own was what she was going to be, for a whole week. "Isn't there some way you could come too?"

Sofie's ears twitched with hope for a second, but then she laid her muzzle on the duvet sadly. "I do not see how, Lottie."

Lottie nibbled a fingernail thoughtfully. "I wonder if Ariadne could show us a spell to make you invisible." She sighed. "No, actually I bet she'd just say something about it being an excellent opportunity to practise speaking to each other from a distance. Which is totally unfair, because Tabitha goes everywhere with her! And Uncle Jack just wouldn't understand; he doesn't have a familiar. He adores everyone in the shop too much to choose."

Sofie gave a sympathetic snort.

"Could you just try being really quiet? If I hid you somehow? We must have to take a big bag of clothes and stuff – if I just took one pair of jeans or something. . ."

"Then you would smell," Sofie pointed out. "Besides, those girls, they said about the mud. In fact, it does not sound like the sort of place at all that I would like. But for you I would go, Lottie."

Lottie kissed her nose. "Could we try an invisibility spell ourselves? Or maybe we could just make you really small. Would that be OK?"

Sofie shook her ears. "That sort of thing — changing people — is very hard, Lottie. I do not think we are ready for that yet. You may have to do this on your own. And you will have Ruby, at least."

Lottie nodded. "I suppose. I just don't want to." She smiled miserably. "This trip is supposed to be fun; it's a treat! Some treat. . ."

Sofie wrinkled her nose. "Be quiet, Lottie, I am having an idea. I need to concentrate. Making someone small. Small. . ." She looked up at Fred, still sitting on a carved wooden swirl on the bed frame, and eyed him speculatively.

"What? What?" Fred twisted around to check that his tail wasn't caught up, and then stared back at her. "Don't look at me like that, it's rude."

Sofie climbed further on to the pillow, her jewel-bright black claws sinking into the softness as she scrambled towards him. "You can go," she told him in a low growl. "You *will* go, and you will look after her, and you will make sure no one hurts her, or I will bite your tail off, mouse! Do you understand me?"

Fred cowered back against the bed, wringing his tail between his paws. "OK! Yes! I promise!"

Sofie nodded. "There," she told Lottie. "At least you will have someone. Better than nothing. Probably." She buried her nose in the crook of Lottie's elbow, and spoke to her silently. *I will be with you all the time, in your thoughts. But it may be hard to hear me, so far away. I do not know.*

"I don't want to go!" Lottie wailed.

Lottie came home from school the day before Year Six were to set off on their activity week, and gloomily set off upstairs to pack.

She found Sofie sitting on her bedroom floor, staring into the kitbag she was taking with her. When Sofie saw Lottie coming in, she wriggled backwards and sniffed. "I thought you might have some chocolate in there," she muttered throatily. But Lottie was sure that she had been wondering if she could fit in the bag – which she could, easily. It would just be too hard to hide her away while they were there. Sofie was not a discreet dog. She liked to be noticed.

Lottie had lined one of the pockets of her little rucksack with soft shredded paper for Fred. He was very excited about the trip, and had been negotiating with Uncle Jack about a supply of mouse brandy for travel sickness. And in case of emergencies. And, of course, some for the journey back.

Now he wriggled importantly into his pocket, and stashed a supply of sunflower seeds in the bottom. He very carefully avoided smirking at Sofie. He might be a flighty little mouse, but he knew when not to push his luck.

Lottie wandered round her room, picking up clothes here and there, and a book, and her pencils, and Sofie watched her all the time with mournful eyes.

At last Lottie sat down on her bed. "It's so far away," she murmured. "I wish we'd tested how far apart we could be and still talk to each other. Do you think since it's magic anyway and it isn't for very long, maybe how far it is won't matter?"

Sofie nodded. "Almost certainly." But she sank her muzzle on to Lottie's leg, and lay there silently for a while.

Chapter 5

Lottie and Ruby had bagged a seat together on the coach, and they were rolling out of Netherbridge, threading their way towards the motorway. "Were Sam and Joe all right this morning?" Ruby asked, offering Lottie a sweet. Ruby had brought the lizards round the night before, so they could spend the week at the pet shop. Ruby's mum was an artist, and a bit ditzy. Ruby had been delighted when Uncle Jack offered to board them for her; at least she knew that they'd get fed that way. Now they were lolling about in a large heated tank, licking their lips and chortling at the horrified faces of the mice.

"They were fine, really," she told Ruby.

"Those monsters! Half my family will have disappeared by the time we get back," Fred told her gloomily, peeping out of his pocket.

"Shh! Or I'll zip you up!" Lottie told him sternly.

"So mean!" Fred gave her a shocked glare.

Lottie sighed and muttered to Ruby, "There's no way he's going to keep hidden all week. This was a bad idea."

Ruby giggled. "To be honest, I think you'll be lucky if we even get there without him deciding to go walkabout! It's a long journey."

"Fred, you have to stay in there!" Lottie whispered, looking at him anxiously. "I promise when we get there you can stay in my coat pocket, and you can look out, as long as you're careful. But you mustn't let anyone see you! Promise?"

Fred sighed. "Oh, very well," he muttered, and flounced back into the pocket, his tail sliding inside like a grumpy little snake.

"Great," Lottie murmured. "Now even the mouse is sulking. Just what I need. I'm not sure I'm going to enjoy this week."

"You're really missing Sofie already, aren't you?" Ruby asked quietly.

"Is it that easy to tell?" Lottie gave her an apologetic look.

Ruby frowned thoughtfully. "There's just something about you. You're all huddled up, like you're cold."

"It feels like that," Lottie agreed, and leant her head sadly against the window.

"There it is!" someone called from the front of the coach, and Lottie jerked awake.

"Are we here?" she asked Ruby, swallowing a yawn. They had been driving for hours, or at least it felt like it.

Ruby nodded. She was peering out of the window past Lottie, and all of a sudden she grabbed Lottie's hand. "Look – that's where we're going! Doesn't it look amazing?"

Broom Manor lay in a little valley below them, and now the coach was slowly winding down a narrow road beside a gushing, foaming stream dotted with tiny waterfalls. The dark, leafless trees hung over the water, and Lottie felt as though they were entering some strange, fairy-tale place. Then she smiled to herself. Six months ago, Lottie would have thought that *she* was something out of a fairy tale.

"It looks very. . ." She trailed off, and then added, "Very wild." It was true. The foaming water and spiky trees made her think of Hansel and Gretel, lost and hungry in the woods. Lottie sighed. She loved going for walks round Netherbridge, and she felt like far more of a country person than she'd ever thought she would be when she first moved there. But she wasn't sure that Broom Manor was going to be her sort of thing. It looked awfully cold and muddy outside the nice warm coach.

"Look at the house," Ruby breathed, practically sitting in Lottie's lap to see.

"Wow," Lottie muttered. It was odd. The house looked as though someone had taken a tourist leaflet about British country houses, cut it up and stuck it back together again. Wrong. There were castley bits, and a Tudor black-and-white bit, and stuck into the middle was a grand flight of steps up to a Georgian front door. A very unimpressed-looking peacock eyed the coach drawing up, and stalked away across the gardens. It was very disappointing to see a boring *All visitors please report to the office* sign, just like at school.

"It looks amazing," Ruby told her excitedly. "Oooh, look, round the back of the house – just behind that funny chimney. Can you see it? That's the abseiling tower, isn't it?"

"Is it?" Lottie gazed at it, her heart thumping nervously. It was enormous. They were supposed to climb down that? She had expected to be miserable and homesick for quite a lot of this week, she just hadn't reckoned on being terrified too. And cold. She shivered as she climbed out of the coach, and she caught a small squeak from her bag about frostbitten paws. She patted the pocket sympathetically.

Mrs Laurence marshalled them efficiently into the house – through a more modern back door, not the smart door by the steps. Lottie had a feeling those steps were only for the peacocks.

They had worked out who was sharing rooms with who back at school the previous week. The rooms were mostly for two people, and a few threes. Lottie and Ruby hadn't even had to consider using magic. Mrs Laurence had simply smiled at them and said she supposed they wanted to go together. It was the one good thing about the week, as far as Lottie could see – it was like a giant sleepover with Ruby.

Those lizards have very bad manners, a grumpy, velvety little voice said in her ear.

Lottie dropped her kitbag halfway up the stairs, and had to run back and fetch it as it slid, making everyone struggling up behind her grumble and call her an idiot.

So you are arrived, then?

Yes, yes. I can hear you!

Well, of course, Lottie, since you are answering me, Sofie sniffed irritably.

Sorry — I'm just so glad. I couldn't hear you — I fell asleep, and then when I woke up I couldn't feel you being there any more.

Is that pink creature behaving himself?

Yes. He's fine. I miss you, though.

Good. There was a distinct sense of satisfaction in the little dog's voice, and Lottie felt Sofie turn round on her velvet cushion in the shop and curl up to sleep, exhausted by the effort of reaching her.

Once Sofie stopped talking, it was as though Lottie tuned in to the rest of the world again. Lots of people were complaining at her, and Zara and her friends were right there in the front.

"She's crazy!" Bethany shook her head in disgust.

"Away with the fairies," Amy giggled.

Lottie blushed. Usually she managed to deal with Sofie inside her head and carry on with whatever else she was supposed to be doing. She had perfected a bright, interested face that she used for school while Sofie told her silly French jokes in the boring bits of lessons. But today she had forgotten all about pretending, and hadn't cared what people thought.

"Really, what else can you expect?" Zara muttered disgustedly, aiming a kick at Lottie's kitbag as she hauled her own smart pink wheelie case up the stairs. "She's crazy, everyone knows. She talks to herself. Not surprising, actually. Ruby's the only other person who'd talk to her. *I'd* rather talk to myself than talk to Ruby Geddis."

"Just ignore her," Ruby muttered, and Lottie felt even worse – she'd got Zara being mean to Ruby, not just herself.

Lily, who was coming up the stairs behind them with Emily, glared after Zara and nodded.

"We can't let them ruin our week."

"Are you feeling homesick?" Emily asked Lottie sympathetically. "I really miss my little sister."

Lottie nodded. She couldn't explain to Emily exactly how, but it was homesickness of a kind. "I miss my dog," she muttered, hoping that didn't sound silly compared to a sister.

"Oh, your cute little dachshund!" Lily smiled. "She's gorgeous. But your mum and dad will look after her, won't they?"

I do not need looking after. Sofie sounded affronted. *And less of the little, if you please.*

Lottie smiled. "She'll be fine. I just miss her, that's all." She was telling Sofie as much as Lily.

Hmf. I am going back to sleep now.

"Mrs Laurence said our room's next to yours. And luckily, it's up the other end of the passage from Little Miss Perfect." Lily eyed Lottie. "Are you OK now? Shall we go and see what the rooms are like?"

They were fantastic, full of odd little nooks and crannies, as they'd been made out of the big bedrooms of the old house. Lottie and Ruby's room had dark oak panelling, and a tiny little window with a big wide sill that they could sit on and watch the peacocks strolling around outside as though they owned the place.

Lottie peered out and sighed. "It's lovely. Almost more beautiful than Netherbridge." She gave a snorting sort of laugh. "I can't believe I just said that. When I arrived in Netherbridge back in the summer, I thought it was a complete dump!"

Ruby nodded. "It is sometimes. Nothing to do, only the same people you've known for ever. But it's beautiful, even when you're sick to death of it." She gazed out at the wintry trees, and the hills rising around the valley. "I love all the water here, though. It's a lot wilder than our river."

Lottie shuddered. "Yes, but have you seen the timetable? We're going canoeing on that!"

"Oh, excellent!" Ruby eyes glittered with excitement, and Lottie eyed her, frowning.

"Are you mad? Ruby, it's December! We're going to freeze to death! It'll be like exploring the Arctic, having to break the ice before we can go anywhere. . ."

Ruby nodded, but she still looked excited. "I suppose, but I've always wanted to try canoeing, whizzing through the water like that, it looks so fun. Like being a – a –"

"A duck?" Lottie suggested, grinning.

Fred scampered up Lottie's arm to sit on her shoulder and leant forwards, pressing his whiskers against the blurred old glass. "We're going to get wet?" he asked in dismay. "We're going out in *that*?"

"In a very small boat," Lottie told him gloomily.

Fred pulled back and shook his whiskers dramatically. "No."

"I think we have to," Lottie explained. "Well, I do. You can stay here, don't worry."

Fred glared up at her with beady black eyes. "Are you trying to trick me, Lottie? Is Sofie listening? You know quite well what she said. I am not to let you out of my sight! Where you go, I go!" He glanced out of the window again, and a shiver ran through him from whiskers to tail. "And we are not going anywhere near that water."

"Tomorrow morning, that's when we're going canoeing." Lottie sighed. "Sorry, Fred. I don't want to either, but we can't get out of it. Think of it like a mud bath – you know, for extra-shiny fur."

"I only like expensive mud." Fred eyed her crossly. "Lottie! Have you no imagination? You're a witch! Do something!"

Lottie blinked. He was right, of course, and she felt rather silly that she hadn't thought of it herself. "But . . . do you think I should? I'm not really supposed to do spells except for good reasons."

Fred leaned closer and scowled, which was quite difficult for a mouse. "Not getting me wet is a *very* good reason!" he hissed.

Chapter 6

The next morning, Lottie was woken early by the tickle of tiny whiskers over her nose. "Lottie! Get up! It's time to do the spell!" Fred was perched on her pillow, looking agitated. His glossy pink fur was his best feature, and the thought of muddy cold water getting anywhere near it was making him even more excitable than usual.

Lottie sat up, yawning, and blinked at Fred. The temptation to tease him was too great to resist. "Do you know, I quite fancy a nice dip in cold water today!" she told him brightly. "It would really wake me up."

Fred gazed at her tragically, his whiskers drooping and losing their sparkle.

Lottie felt guilty. "I'm sorry, I'm sorry, I'm only teasing. Come on."

She grabbed her warm jumper from the chair and slipped it on. Broom Manor was beautiful but chilly. Lots of the girls had complained about the useless showers the night before. Apparently the water had run freezing cold right after Zara had shampooed her hair.

Lottie curled up on the window sill, shivering as her skin touched the frosted glass. She blew on it, rubbing a little hole to see out through the leafy patterns, and huddled closer into her jumper.

I am deliciously warm, a smug little voice told her, and Lottie sighed. *Don't gloat, Sofie, it's mean. I was going to bring you a bar of Kendal Mint Cake from the shop, but I won't if you're horrible.*

I would prefer chocolate. And a wave of velvety warmth suddenly rushed over Lottie, as though Sofie had blown on her.

Thanks!

Even Fred felt it. He stopped rubbing his

tail and moaning, and gave a relieved little sigh.

Do the spell with him, Lottie. He is clever – for a mouse. I can send warm love, but I cannot reach far enough to help you with magic. Sofie's voice in her mind had dropped to a sad whisper.

"I'll be back soon," Lottie promised out loud. It felt more definite that way.

"Sofie says you're clever," she told Fred, smiling.

Fred blinked. "She wants something," he muttered grimly. "I don't want to be indebted to a dog. Why is she being nice? She never normally is."

"She's relying on you." Lottie stroked the top of his head gently. "Her magic won't reach this far – or only for tiny things, like warming us up. She can't do the spell with us. She needs you. Like I do."

Fred swayed slightly, his eyes wide. "You need me?" he murmured happily. "Really? Like a proper useful mouse? Almost a familiar?"

74

"Almost." Lottie nodded.

"We must do the spell *now*," Fred told her importantly. "Before anyone else wakes up and sees us. How are we going to do it? Can I do something? Can I?"

Lottie scratched a little more of the frost off the windowpane, building a tiny pile of frost shavings in the palm of her hand and letting the warmth of her skin melt them to nothing, to a few tiny drops of water. She shook her hand gently, letting the water spread over her skin, running into the lines and cracks of her palm.

"Dabble your whiskers in it," she told Fred, and he did.

"Ugh, it's still chilly," he muttered, sitting up with watery diamonds spangling his whiskers.

"It won't be for long," Lottie promised. She closed her eyes, imagining her skin smooth and dry, and Fred's fur oiled, so that the water ran off it.

The droplets shivered and ran up the side of her hand, seeping away on to the window sill. Fred's whiskers were dry.

"Was that it?" he asked, sounding rather disappointed.

Lottie nodded. "We're waterproof now." She blinked. "Ugh, I should have cleaned my teeth first."

Surprisingly, the canoeing was fun. It would have been less fun if Lottie had had to worry about the boys, who kept paddling up and trying to splash everyone, but her spell meant that the water shook itself away from her in sparkling droplets.

"Did you do something, you and Fred?" Ruby whispered, paddling closer. "Everyone else is wet. Look at Emily!" Emily had capsized her canoe and was clambering out on the muddy bank of the lake, allowed to go back to the house and get dry. Lottie thought she might have tipped over on purpose.

"We did – Fred was really upset about getting wet." She glanced down at her coat pocket, where Fred was peeping out. He beamed at Ruby.

"Your hair is quite a different colour when it's wet! You're not ginger any more!" he told her brightly, and Ruby huffed.

Even without getting wet, it was still cold, and Lottie was glad to go back inside after an hour. Everyone looked damp, even Zara, although she didn't seem to care. She had charmed the canoeing instructor the way she did with all the teachers. Lottie had to admit that she had actually been very good at canoeing. She was a sporty sort of person. Now she was looking around pityingly at the rest of the class, who looked like drowned rats and kept moaning that they were freezing.

"Look at her. How does she manage to still look perfect, even though she's got half a river down her neck?" Ruby asked.

"Natural talent, I think," Lottie sighed. "I

hadn't realized she was an outdoors sort of person."

"Oh, you must have heard her going on about her expensive pony-trekking holidays!"

Lottie nodded. "Mmm. I always thought she just sat on the pony and it took her to the next nice hotel, though."

Ruby chuckled, and Zara heard them. Her dark-blue eyes looked them over, and her face settled into a pitying sort of sneer. "Lottie, did you hide under a bush on the riverbank or something? You aren't even wet."

Lottie shrugged. "I was just lucky."

Zara's eyes narrowed, and Lottie had a feeling that she might not be allowed to get away with just lucky next time.

Broom Manor was set up for all sorts of outdoor activities, and there was a packed schedule. Whenever they weren't swimming (in an indoor pool, thank goodness) or climbing rope courses, or swinging off zip wires, Lottie's class had drama workshops and team bonding. That was particularly embarrassing, and Mrs Laurence loved it. Lily swore to Emily, Lottie and Ruby that she'd heard Mrs Laurence asking the manager to fit in extra sessions because it was such fun.

"She didn't! I can't possibly play Twister while I talk about my feelings again. It's torture!" Ruby's hair had been wet so often over the last few days that it was standing almost straight upwards in corkscrew curls, and now they bounced in horror.

Lottie nodded. She didn't want to talk about her feelings, in case she made a complete idiot of herself and started crying. She *was* having a good time, but underneath the fun, she missed Sofie so much. She blinked, feeling inside her mind for Sofie.

"Just going to the loo," she muttered to the others, but she ran straight past the loos and made for the long gallery along from the TV room, where there were big curtained window sills. Where she could hide, just for a minute.

You are there!

I had to talk to you. I felt so lonely all of a sudden. Are you all right, Sofie?

Of course I am, silly girl. But her thoughts sounded wistful. *You are home soon?*

Two more days. This big expedition walk thing tomorrow, and then we come home on Friday. Only two days.

"Lottie! Why are you hiding behind a curtain?" It was Zara's voice, confident and laughing, and there was a chorus of sniggering behind her.

Lottie felt Sofie snuffle a kiss against her cheek, and then she was gone, her warm furry love slipping away. Lottie swung round to stare at Zara, hating her suddenly, in a way she never had before.

There was a flash of fright in Zara's eyes as Lottie jumped down from the window sill and stood glaring at her, her fingernails digging into her palms. She felt as though Sofie had been torn away from her, and it was all Zara's fault.

Zara gave a sneery laugh, but she took a step back too, and led the others away, laughing loudly at how strange Lottie Grace was.

Lottie raced up to the safety of her room and sank down on to the floor, wrapping her arms around her knees. She felt lost and stupidly alone, even though she knew that Ruby and her other friends were only downstairs. She wanted to go home so much. She had promised Sofie only two days, making it sound like almost nothing, but it wasn't nothing. She couldn't bear the thought of two more nights without Sofie, and the constant hum of love and companionship from all the animals in the shop.

Delicate pinprick claws skittered over her hands, and she opened her eyes to see Fred, his nose about a centimetre away from her own. He was watching her worriedly.

"Oh, Lottie. . ." It came out as a breathy

little squeak. "Those girls. So horrible. Are you all right?"

Lottie smiled tightly at him. "It wasn't them. Or not much, anyway. I just really miss Sofie." She blinked apologetically, realizing it wasn't the most tactful thing to say to Sofie's stand-in.

But he nodded. "I miss her too," he said unexpectedly. "She's always terribly rude to me, but she drops chocolate crumbs."

Lottie giggled, and Fred leant forward a little more, nuzzling her cheek with his velvet nose. His whiskers fizzed against her skin, and she couldn't help but smile.

"You're a very good cheerer-upper," she murmured.

"It really is only two days," Fred promised her. "Less than that, really. We'll be home on Friday afternoon. It isn't long." But his voice sounded deliberately brave, and Lottie knew that he wanted to be home too.

Chapter 7

"Lottie, are you OK?"

Lottie looked up as someone put their arms around her.

"Stupid question. Of course you're not." Ruby hugged her tight, looking down at her worriedly.

"Was it Zara?" Emily asked, sounding worried.

Lottie nodded.

"There's a surprise," Ruby muttered.

"We realized we hadn't seen you in a bit," Lily explained, patting Lottie's arm. "And then Zara and her lot came in looking all pleased with themselves. We thought we should come and look for you."

"She's always worse to you and Ruby because you don't act like sheep and follow her around doing whatever she wants," Emily told Lottie. "Like we did before you came along, Lottie. We'd never have dared stand up to her. *Please* don't let her get to you."

Lottie gave a watery smile and nodded. "I'll try," she promised. And a very long way away, she could feel a velvety, chocolatey rush of pride, as Sofie heard her.

"It's true, you know." The voice came from the other bed, and Lottie jolted awake again. She hadn't really been asleep, just dozing in the dark, wishing she had Sofie curled comfily by her knees. Fred was blissfully asleep in one of her socks (a clean one, he had insisted, and even then he had complained that it wasn't a hundred per cent cotton; he said artificial fibres gave his fur static). Mrs Laurence had told them to put their lights out ages ago, but that didn't mean they couldn't talk, if they were careful.

"What is?" Lottie asked sleepily, rolling to

the side of her bed and peering over at Ruby, curled up in the other bed. Her eyes were having to get used to the dark again, and Ruby was just a pale smudge in the grey.

"What Emily said. Zara was much worse before you came along. I know it was partly because she picked on me most of the time, and now she does it to you too. We get to share the meanness. . ." Ruby yawned. "But that spell you did on her, when you made everyone see what she's really like, it's still working. A bit."

"It shouldn't be." Lottie blinked worriedly. "I made everyone forget, or I was supposed to. Otherwise they might get suspicious."

Ruby chuckled. "It was too good to forget. Oh, don't worry. No one really remembers, not properly. There's just something sort of lurking at the back of their minds. Something that tells them they don't have to be so terrified of Zara after all."

"What confuses me," Lottie murmured,

rolling back and staring up at the ceiling, "is how she does it. Why are we all so scared of her?"

Ruby was silent for a moment – long enough that Lottie wondered if she'd gone to sleep, but she must just have been thinking. "Well. . . She's pretty. Which means everyone thinks she's special. And she has Bethany and the others with her all the time, and they act like she's amazing, so everyone thinks she is."

"There must be more than that."

"Mmm. I suppose she's good at finding exactly the worst possible thing to say – sometimes I think she's a mind-reader." There was a sudden scuffle, and Lottie realized it was Ruby sitting up. "She isn't, is she?"

"I don't know." Lottie had rolled right to the edge of her bed now. This felt like something they should be close up and whispering about.

"It would explain a lot," Ruby said

thoughtfully. "Ever such a lot. But wouldn't you know if there was another witch in Netherbridge?"

"If she is a witch, I don't think *she* knows. Maybe she just has a little bit of magic."

"Huh. Well, I hope she never realizes. Imagine what she'd do with it." Ruby lay down again with a thump.

Lottie sniffed disgustedly. "Don't, I can't bear to think about it." She yawned again. "Although if anyone round here's got magic, it's you. . ." Her voice trailed off.

Ruby stared at her in the darkness – but Lottie was asleep.

Lottie woke up the next morning to find Ruby sitting on the end of her bed, stroking Fred.

Lottie realized, as she gradually came to, that she could sense a strange worried feeling. Almost as though there was a smell of worry in the air. Something was wrong with Ruby. Lottie peered at her friend, sneaking a glance under her eyelashes. Ruby was still fussing over Fred, rubbing behind his ears, and she wasn't looking at Lottie. But there was no obvious sign that she was upset, just this odd feeling. . .

Lottie decided to stop wondering and just ask.

"What's wrong?"

Ruby looked up, startled. It made her freckles stand out, especially across the bridge of her nose, as though someone had flicked a brush full of brown paint at her. "How did you know? Lottie, you can't read minds as well, can you? Like we thought Zara might?" She folded her arms protectively across her stomach. "Because that isn't fair – you should have said!"

"I can't!" Lottie shook her head. "Honestly. But your face looks absolutely white with worry."

"Oh, I see. . ." Ruby leaned back against the bedroom wall and sighed. "How asleep were you last night, when we were talking?"

Lottie blinked. It wasn't a question that seemed to make sense. "Um. I don't know?" she said hesitantly.

"It was when we were talking about Zara. You said you thought I had magic in me." Ruby stared at Lottie, her eyes a dark, murky, anxious sort of green. "Did you mean it, or were you asleep? You wouldn't say anything after that, you just snored."

"I don't snore!" Lottie protested.

"You do," Fred pronounced, "but only a little bit, Lottie, don't worry."

"The snoring isn't important." Ruby waved this away.

"I really don't," Lottie whispered. "Sorry. Go on."

"Did you mean it about the magic? Or was it one of those random things people say when they're nearly asleep?"

Lottie frowned. "To be honest, I don't remember saying it, so probably I was asleep.

But it's true, anyway." She was watching Ruby's face – which was switching from worried to hopeful to scared and back again. Lottie sighed. She definitely couldn't read minds. It was very hard to tell whether Ruby was happy about the news or not.

"Don't you want to be able to?"

"I just don't know!" Ruby picked at her pyjamas worriedly. "It would be fun, but. . . Well, scary things have happened to you, Lottie. *Really* scary things. Mad enchantresses, and that sort of stuff. . ."

Lottie nodded. "I know. But it's so exciting – not when people like Pandora are trying to turn you into something horrible, of course. But the rest of it, Ruby, learning spells, and meeting all these amazing creatures." She stared at her friend, a tiny frown creasing her forehead. How could anybody not want to be part of that?

Ruby sighed. "Lottie, I love it at the pet shop, seeing all the animals and being around the magic. I've never felt the slightest bit magical, though. I just . . . well, I just watch. . ." She shrugged helplessly.

"It's a lot more fun to do it yourself," Lottie promised her. "Honestly."

"But I don't see what makes you suddenly think I can do it too!" Ruby argued. "Like I said, I've never had tingly fingers, or any of those things you talk about. And I haven't got a familiar."

"Neither's Uncle Jack!" Lottie argued. "He has all the animals in the shop. You don't need just one. And anyway, what about Sam and Joe? They'd love it."

Ruby laughed. "They'd be over the moon. Sometimes I wonder if they'd be happier living at the shop all the time. They love being around magic."

"They love *you*," Lottie assured her. "Really. They chose you, didn't they? They could have had anyone in that huge pet shop. They bothered to work all that magic to persuade you to take them home – and even if you didn't take much work, your mum certainly did."

Ruby nodded doubtfully. "I suppose."

"That's one of the things that makes me wonder if there's magic deep down in you. They must have sensed something, to make them so determined you were the one they wanted to keep them."

Ruby smiled, leaning her chin on her knees and looking dreamy. "They are so cool, aren't they?" she asked Lottie wistfully. "I know you're missing Sofie like mad, and it isn't quite the same – I don't have magic tying me to Sam and Joe – but I do miss them. Although it's quite nice getting up in the morning here without Joe stomping up and down my back. He's always starving by half-past six, and now they can get out of their tank he doesn't see why he ought to wait for breakfast. Mum's really confused about what I do to my pyjama tops – he's ripped three of them. I had to convince her the washing machine just doesn't like me."

Lottie nodded. "You see? That's not like normal pets, Ruby. Sam and Joe mean more to you than that. I think they're halfway to being your familiars already. Look, I'm not saying you have to suddenly start doing complicated spells, or anything like that – but you never know. I bet you might be able to do little things if you wanted."

Ruby said nothing, but her face was thoughtful.

"Right. You've got two hours, everyone, to make your way back to the meeting point." Ben, the expedition leader, was standing next to the minibus, waving a sheaf of maps, which were already curling in the damp, mizzly air. "Now I'll just hand this out to each group."

"Where's the meeting point?" Lottie muttered out of the side of her mouth to Ruby.

There was a dull ache of longing for Sofie in the back of her head, and it was making her feel sick.

"Back at the house." Ruby shook her head. "Are you all right?"

Lottie just shrugged apologetically, and Ruby gave her a quick hug.

"Mind me!" Luckily, Fred's urgent, whispery squeak blended into the chatter from everyone around.

"Now, girls, let's mix these groups up a bit. This week is all about teamwork and learning to work together, after all." Mrs Laurence bustled around, her bright red waterproof making her look like some strange enormous ladybird. "So, Lottie. . ."

"I have to stay with Ruby!" Lottie's voice, sharp and panicked, seemed to break through Mrs Laurence's busy organizing.

She gave Lottie a thoughtful look and nodded. "I know, Lottie."

"Wow, was that a spell?" Ruby murmured

in Lottie's ear.

Lottie shook her head. "No. I think she could just see I really meant it." She gave Ruby a shamefaced smile. "I didn't even think of a spell. Some witch I am."

Mrs Laurence glanced cheerfully around the huddle of damp children. "So . . . Lottie and Ruby, yes . . . let's put you with Amy and Zara."

"Oh no. . ." Ruby whispered.

Lottie's eyes widened, and she desperately tried to think of something, anything, to say, a charm to change minds, or a forgetfulness spell. But her mind felt full of fog. *It's being away from Sofie. A spell to prevent total and utter disaster, that's what I need now. . .* she thought to herself. But Mrs Laurence had already gone on, joining Lily and Emily with Bethany and Ellie, and leaving the four members of Lottie's group glaring at one another, like a gang of furious cats.

"I'll take that, thank you!" Zara snatched

the map from Ruby's hand. "I don't want to end up halfway to Scotland because *you're* in charge, Ruby."

"Actually, we're supposed to work together, you know," Ruby snarled back. "Sharing. Not that it's a concept you'd understand."

"I wouldn't work with you if you paid me." Zara smirked. "You can follow us, I suppose, if you must. At a distance, please. I wouldn't want the wildlife to think you were something to do with me."

Ruby looked around for Mrs Laurence, but Zara was in her face lightning-fast. "Don't," she snapped. "Or you'll regret it. If you think I've been mean to you before, just wait and see what happens if you tell."

"Oh, just follow her, like she says," Lottie muttered wearily. She didn't really care about map-reading. "If she wants to do all the work, we can enjoy the walk. It's amazing up here."

The centre staff had driven them up to one

of the hills around the valley, the minibus bouncing over the rutted track.

"It's the back of beyond," Ruby sighed as Zara and Amy stalked away, flaunting the map. "Look, you can see the house down there, with the stream leading down to it. It looks like a dolls' house, it's so tiny."

"How far do you think it is?" Lottie asked, as they set off down the path with all the other groups. Everyone was squabbling over the maps. The house did seem worryingly small and far away, even though it was beautiful. The wintry fields and patches of woodland had the look of a jigsaw.

"Six kilometres, that's what Ben said." Ruby shrugged. "It isn't that far. I've walked more than that loads of times with my dad. Although then I didn't have the ice princess map-reading," she added darkly.

"It looks like we could just follow this stream down." Lottie pointed along the line of the little stream, which was bouncing and sparkling over the rocks. Further down it widened out and led into the lake where they'd been canoeing, close to the house. "Look, was that a fish?" They crouched on a smooth, round rock at the water's edge, staring in among the weeds.

"You're right, I bet we could just follow this," Ruby agreed. "Although – would they have given us a map if it was that simple?"

Lottie sighed. "I suppose we ought to catch up Zara and Amy then." The other two girls were visible a way in front, peering down at the map and pointing. Lottie and Ruby trotted after them.

Zara turned round, smirking at them, and then sped off.

"She's really starting to annoy me now," Lottie said crossly. "And I don't think this is the right way. If we're going the right way, where's everybody else? We can't have wasted that much time fighting with her, can we? How can they be so far ahead of us that we can't even see them?"

Ruby blinked. "I can't see the stream any more either. I can hear it, I think. Over there?"

Fred nosed his way out of Lottie's pocket, and sniffed the air. "Yes. Over there, for definite. It smells cold."

Lottie and Ruby exchanged worried glances. The countryside was beautiful, but that didn't mean they wanted to be stuck out in it for any longer than necessary.

"We need to have a look at that map," Ruby muttered. "Zara's so stubborn, if she's made a mistake she'll never admit it; she'll just keep on going." She set off at a run down the narrow path on the edge of the hillside towards Zara and Amy, two small figures close to a tumble of craggy rocks.

"Slow down," Lottie said anxiously. "If you trip you'll go straight down on to those rocks."

Ruby nodded, and yelled down at Zara and Amy instead. "Hey! You're going the wrong way!"

Zara looked back at her. "No, we're not."

Lottie and Ruby slid carefully down the steep hillside towards the other two, and skidded to a halt next to them on the rocky ledge. Lottie tried to look at the map, but Zara held it behind her back, like a toddler with a toy.

"Oh, grow up!" Lottie snapped. "We're nowhere near where we should be. Let us look."

"I know exactly where we are," Zara said stubbornly. But Lottie could feel a tiny smidgeon of doubt wavering around her. Zara *wasn't* sure, even if she wouldn't admit it to herself.

"Let us see!" Lottie tried to snatch the map, darting behind Zara, but Zara only twirled on the spot, jeering. "Come on, then! Try and get it!" And she gave Lottie a shove.

A shove which completely unbalanced Lottie, who was still reaching out for the map, and sent her sprawling over the edge of the path.

"Lottie! Are you OK?" Ruby leaned out after her. "Oh no!"

Lottie was stuck on a little rocky outcrop about two metres below the path, curled up and clutching her foot, which had doubled under her as she fell.

"Fred! Fred!" Lottie didn't care that Zara and Amy were there, staring white-faced over the rocks at her. What if he was hurt?

But a small pink nose appeared out of her pocket, the whiskers trembling. "Lottie, never pick a fight on the side of a mountain," Fred squeaked, his eyes popping slightly with panic.

"It isn't a mountain," Lottie whispered back. "Well, only a bit of one. I didn't mean to, I'm sorry. She was just being so stupid."

"Are you hurt?" Ruby called.

"I've banged my foot." Lottie tried getting up. "Ow. Owww. I can stand on it, but it really hurts."

"You shouldn't have been fighting!" Amy accused her shrilly. "You pushed Zara!"

"She did not!" Ruby turned on Amy, yelling. "You saw it, don't lie! Zara pushed her over the edge, and I don't care what you do to people who tell, Zara. There's no way I'm not telling *everyone* about this."

Lottie was hardly listening. A wave of sudden panic had washed over her, as Sofie felt that she was hurt and in danger.

What is happening? Where are you? That mouse, I tell him, I made him swear to look after you. Lottie!

I'm all right, honestly.

You are stuck.

Lottie could almost feel Sofie pacing around the shop, sniffing and growling as she tried to get a sense of what was going on so far away.

"You have to help me pull her up!" Lottie vaguely heard Ruby arguing with Zara and Amy. Pull her up – that sounded sensible. Sofie was really worried because she couldn't see what was going on properly, and that made it hard for Lottie to concentrate.

"Lottie, grab my coat." A sleeve was dangling down in front of her.

"Lottie!" Fred had scrambled up inside her waterproof, and now he was balanced on her shoulder. "Lottie, come on. You have to try and climb up!"

Lottie nodded muzzily, and put her left foot, the one that didn't hurt, on to a rock, pulling against Ruby's jacket to try and lever herself up. But she couldn't get a grip on it and she slid back down, landing painfully on her bruised foot again and crying out.

Fred leapt clear of her shoulder, springing on to a clump of grass that was anchored in the rocks. Then he ran round the grass, leaving a glittery pink trail, one that Lottie could only see if she tilted her head at just the right angle. "What are you doing?" she murmured.

"Making a ladder for you. Poor humans never can climb properly." Fred knotted two blades of grass together with delicate paws, and bit through another.

"How did you know how to do that. . ." Lottie blinked. The pink traces did seem to form a ladder – even if it was a wobbly-looking one.

"We mice are good at climbing." Fred scampered higher, shoving stones this way and that, and nibbling roots. Then he leapt back to Lottie's shoulder. "Now try climbing again. Start with that tuft of grass."

Lottie nodded, reaching out and grabbing it. It seemed to wriggle and grow in her fingers, gripping them tight, and Lottie could feel Fred somehow pulling her up – or was he pushing? Neither, since he was sitting on her shoulder, but she could feel strong little paws, helping her up. . .

Wearily, Lottie wriggled over the lip of the overhang, Ruby dragging her by the arms, and even Amy helping. Only Zara stood there glaring suspiciously.

"How did you suddenly get up there? You

were totally stuck! You fell back down after about two steps the first time you tried. Were you faking?" Suddenly Zara crouched down next to Lottie, who was nursing her aching foot and grimacing.

Fred had snuggled back into her pocket, and she patted him, still sensing those pink shimmers.

Zara's eyes were a strange, hard blue, and her mouth was set in a suspicious twist, as though she could tell that something was going on, she just couldn't quite pin it down. "And what's that in your pocket?" she snapped. "You keep stroking your pocket. What is it?"

"Nothing!" Lottie snapped. Why couldn't everyone just leave her alone? The pain in her foot was making her feel dizzy and bad-tempered.

Ruby was yelling at Zara, and Fred was wriggling worriedly inside her pocket. Lottie wished that she could speak to him silently, the way she did with Sofie. She needed to tell

him that she would never let Zara hurt him —
but she couldn't, not without making it
obvious that there *was* something she was
hiding. She really didn't want Zara and Amy
knowing that she was carrying around a
magical pink mouse.

It hit her suddenly that telling Fred not to
worry would be deeply stupid. He *should*
worry. Lottie could hardly think, let alone
stop Zara. She scrambled backwards, away
from Zara's grasping fingers, but Zara was
standing up now, and she wasn't held back by
an injured foot. She jumped after Lottie and
grabbed at her pocket. There was a faint but
audible squeak, and Zara's eyes flashed with
triumph as she grabbed again. "It's something
from that stupid shop! You've brought a pet
with you! You're going to get in so much
trouble, Lottie!" Her voice rang with glee at
the thought.

"Leave her alone!" Ruby yelled, and from
inside Lottie's pocket came a threatening

growl, far louder than any sound Fred should have been able to make. It echoed eerily around the rocks, and even Lottie shivered a little.

The effect on Zara was immediate. The bright flush of excitement on her cheeks died away, and she scrambled along the path, holding Amy half in front of her.

"What *is* that?" she whispered.

Lottie tried hard to look threatening, which was difficult when half of her wanted to laugh and the other half was whimpering about how much her foot hurt. "You don't want to know. . ." she muttered. Next to her Ruby folded her arms and gave a threatening nod.

Zara and Amy vanished down the path, Zara glancing back over her shoulder. "We're telling!" she announced, in a high, frightened voice.

Fred wriggled out of Lottie's pocket and snuggled up on her shoulder, and Ruby sat down next to her and smirked. "I'm really sorry your foot hurts, but you have to admit that was funny."

Lottie shook her head. "Yes and no. Because she's on her way back to the house now, isn't she? And it's going to be *Oh, Mrs Laurence, Lottie and Ruby were so mean to us, and they wouldn't let us look at the map, and Lottie got in a fight with me about it.*"

Ruby sighed. "You're right. I suppose it doesn't solve anything. But it was worth it to see her face, Lottie, to be honest."

Lottie grinned. "I know what you mean. She deserved it."

Fred snorted. "She deserves a lot more!" He brushed his whiskers rather smugly. "It was a good noise, though, wasn't it? Really scary?"

"You were magnificent," Lottie told him lovingly. "How did you do it?"

Fred shrugged. "Oh, it was nothing. It's all in the voice projection," he said airily. "The diaphragm, you know. . ." Then he added seriously, "Someone needs to deal with that girl properly. Once and for all."

Ruby nodded. "Sounds good to me. But I thought you weren't supposed to go around attracting attention with this magic thing?"

"I'll think about it," Fred muttered darkly. "She'd just better watch out."

It took Lottie and Ruby a lot longer than the two hours to get back to the house. Lottie's foot was swelling up inside her welly, and it hurt to walk, even after Fred had run glittery whiskers over it, sending her all his magic. He was already worn out from the ladder spell and scaring Zara, and eventually he sat down on her foot, looking annoyed with himself.

"It isn't working," he admitted with a sigh.

"Fred, you'd better hide, someone's coming," Ruby muttered, staring down the path. As Zara and Amy had disappeared with the map, she and Lottie were following the stream, and they'd managed to get as far as the canoeing lake.

"Girls! Where on earth have you been?" Mrs Laurence was striding towards them with Ben, and they both looked angry.

"Lottie hurt her foot, Mrs Laurence," Ruby protested.

"And I've just had Zara telling me some mad story about you having an animal with you, Lottie. I can't believe that's true, but apparently you were also pushing her on the side of the hill! Why on earth were you fighting over the map with her?" Mrs Laurence demanded. "What a stupid way to behave!"

"She wouldn't let us see it. . ." Lottie faltered, realizing that Zara had probably only told the truth, or some twisted version of it. She *had* tried to grab the map off Zara, after all. She lapsed into silence, unsure what to say. Her head still felt like marshmallow, and her foot was aching miserably.

Ruby gave her an anxious look and put an arm around her. Lottie had told Ruby she couldn't read her mind, but she could feel the worry seeping out of her friend. "I'm all right," she muttered.

"And you, Ruby! I know you don't get on with Zara, but I'm surprised at you! Zara says that you two really hurt her."

Ruby took a deep breath. "Neither of us touched her, Mrs Laurence." Which was true, too.

"If we weren't going home tomorrow, I would ask your parents to come and fetch you," Mrs Laurence snapped. "As it is, you can miss the disco tonight."

Ruby raised her eyebrows at Lottie, just a smidge, and Lottie managed a small smile, hardly more than a quirk of her lips. Did Mrs Laurence really think that missing the lame disco was such an awful punishment? They'd had one on the first night, and Lottie could do without another hour of watching the boys snigger and point.

"Mrs Laurence. . ." Ruby tried to break in,

as Mrs Laurence continued scolding. "Mrs Laurence, Lottie really needs to sit down!"

Mrs Laurence glared at Ruby, but Ruby glared back, strengthened by the tiny pink mouse who had scrambled across from Lottie's shoulder and was now sitting in the hood of Ruby's waterproof jacket and coiling little pink sparks into her red curls.

"We'd better get her back to the house," Ben agreed. "The minibus is just over here, girls."

"Well, I do hope this shows you two how silly and irresponsible you've been," Mrs Laurence told them crossly.

"Sorry, Mrs Laurence," Ruby murmured, trying to sound meek, as they were shepherded into the minibus.

"Thanks for standing up for me," Lottie whispered to her, as they drove off.

Ruby nodded. "Are you feeling any better?"

Lottie nodded, still white-faced. "I still feel sick, but now I think I could manage to wait until we're back, just in case there's a chance to throw up on Zara's shoes," she muttered weakly.

Their whole class were watching, eager for more drama, as the bus pulled up outside the house. Lottie could see Zara, blue eyes washed with tears, surrounded by the other girls, and obviously acting the injured party.

She didn't care. In fact, Lottie was beginning to think Fred was quite right. It was time to remind everyone what Zara was really like.

Chapter 8

"Not one of them will come out and help! Can you believe that? What is the matter with them? Useless! Completely useless!" Fred stomped up and down the bedroom floor in front of a hole in the skirting board, his tail swirling dramatically behind him. "The mice in this part of the country must be particularly cowardly," he snapped.

"Have you really never met a – a – normal mouse before?" Lottie stared up at him, trying not to laugh – partly because it would upset him even more, but also because her foot still ached if she moved too much. She was lying on her bed with a bag of frozen sweetcorn from the kitchen on her foot. It looked as though someone had blown it up like a balloon, but apparently she had only twisted it.

"Normal! They're not normal! *I'm* normal!" Fred shrieked. "They are unbelievably stupid, backwards and – and *beige*!"

Ruby couldn't stop herself laughing at that, and Lottie had to bite the back of her hand. "Beige?" she spluttered.

"A horrible, boring, nothing colour. Greyish beige, at that." Fred sat down huffily. "It isn't funny, Lottie. I was expecting them to help! They just didn't seem to understand me. And I used small words."

"I don't think mice usually understand any words at all," Lottie explained. "They're mostly just thinking about finding food."

"Well, that I can understand," Fred muttered. "I'm running very low on sunflower seeds, Lottie, and the muesli this place provides is distinctly substandard."

Ruby threw one of the paper aeroplanes she'd been making at Fred, but it missed. "Hey, don't moan, Fred. I had to spill milk all over our table this morning to distract people while Lottie nicked you some more muesli. Mrs Laurence had a go at me in front of everyone."

Fred sighed, and nibbled thoughtfully at the paper aeroplane. Then he spat it out, his whiskers quivering in disgust. "Yuck. I can force the muesli down, I suppose. But I want the best demerara sugar lumps when we get home, Lottie, a week's supply." His whiskers twitched crossly. "I'm sure I could think better if there was sugar," he moaned. "If the mice here won't help, then I suppose I shall have to do it myself."

"Do what?" Lottie asked uncertainly. Fred's eyes were glittering in a rather worrying way. He looked like he'd had far too much sugar already, and since she *knew* there wasn't any, that meant he was just overexcited. . .

"I'm going to introduce dear Zara to mice. One mouse, actually. I was planning to use a volunteer, but it seems I shall have to do it myself, which will of course mean that it's a virtuoso performance."

"When you say introduce. . ." Lottie began.

"I'm going to wake her up in the middle of the night." Fred stroked his whiskers smugly. "By sitting on her duvet and chewing her hair. If I can bring myself to. I suppose it's a good thing I'm starving."

"She'll go mad!" Ruby whispered.

"Exactly. And then everyone will see her making a complete fool of herself over a tiny little brown mouse. I shall have to go brown for the night, which will be a hardship, of course, but there are times, Lottie, when a mouse knows his duty, even if it means wearing out-of-season colours."

Lottie nodded, savouring the thought. "Is she scared of mice, do we know?" she asked Ruby.

"Oh yes." Ruby grinned. "The only animals she likes are horses. And she's always moaning about how she's sure there are rats at that posh stables she goes to."

"I will be the most adorable little mouse anyone has ever seen, and she will look cruel and horrible because she's screaming at me." Fred allowed his whiskers to tremble winningly, and tried hard to look helpless. It didn't really work – he couldn't stop giggling.

"You'd better be careful," Lottie pointed out, feeling suddenly worried. "What if she tries to squash you?"

Fred eyed her pityingly. "Lottie, have you ever tried to squash a mouse?"

"Of course not! But Zara might do it!"

Fred simply sniggered. "Not a chance. Can you turn me brown, Lottie?"

"I can try," Lottie said doubtfully. She simply couldn't imagine Fred as a brown mouse. She held out her hand and he climbed into it, holding out his paws to see the colour of his fur.

"A *nice* brown, Lottie. Toffee-coloured. Not too greyish."

"I'm doing my best!" Lottie murmured, with her eyes closed. Now that Fred had mentioned toffee, she kept imagining him as a toffee mouse, or maybe a furry little fudge Fred. She smiled to herself, combing out fudgy-coloured fur in her head. It seemed to work quite well as a spell, especially as Fred had always reminded her of a pink sugar mouse anyway. "There! Is that good enough?"

"Ugh. It doesn't suit me at all," Fred wailed. "I look old."

"I think it's a very pretty colour," Ruby told him comfortingly, but Fred threw her a look of such scornful disbelief that she stopped trying to be nice.

"You still don't really look like a normal mouse." Lottie frowned. She couldn't really pin it down. Perhaps it was the slight shimmer on Fred's glossy, sugary-brown fur if you caught it at the right angle. Or the way his whiskers still looked like a silvery waterfall.

"I should hope not." Fred shuddered. "But it'll do. What time is it?"

"Nine o'clock. I suppose we should get ready for bed. Mrs Laurence's bound to come and check on us."

"Only nine!" Fred's whiskers drooped. "I was planning to wait until midnight; that's ages. Are you sure it's only nine, Lottie?" He peered at her watch, upside down. "Is that definitely going?" he demanded suspiciously.

"I promise it is," Lottie assured him. "Why don't you have a sleep? You know, make sure you're ready for your big performance."

Fred shook his head. "I couldn't possibly. The adrenaline, you know. It's already flowing. I shall do some vocal warm-up exercises, so I can manage a really loud squeak." He retired under Ruby's bed, and the girls tried not to laugh as a succession of tiny growls and mewing sounds echoed around the room.

What is that idiot mouse doing? And are you all right, Lottie cherie?

I'm fine! I've got ice on my foot – it doesn't really hurt. He's practising, so he can go and frighten Zara. He wants to get revenge on her for this afternoon.

At last he shows some sense, Sofie muttered. *I shall watch with you. Midnight, huh?*

Yes. And then it will actually be tomorrow. Lottie sighed.

Do not be sentimental, Lottie. Sofie's tone was brisk, like being rubbed with a rough towel. *But you are not going away again any time soon, are you?* she added, rather spoiling the effect.

Never, if I can help it, Lottie promised. *Oh! I think Fred's fallen asleep!*

"Lottie! Lottie, wake up! Why did you go to sleep? Oh, wake up!"

Lottie shook herself awake to find Fred on her pillow. "Oh, hello!"

"It's nearly midnight! What did you go to sleep for?"

"Well, you went to sleep, so Ruby and I thought—"

"I did not! I've been awake all evening!" Fred looked so indignant that Lottie decided it probably wasn't worth arguing with him.

"Sorry! So, are you ready to go?" Lottie sank her voice to a whisper, feeling like a conspirator. "Shall I wake up Ruby?"

"I'm awake," Ruby muttered sleepily. "What are we going to do, wait outside in the corridor?"

"Too obvious." Fred shook his head. "You don't want people thinking you had anything to do with it. Just be ready to run out as soon as you hear screaming, and perhaps make a bit of a fuss. Wish me luck." He brushed his whiskers over Lottie's cheek in a mouse kiss and slid down the side of her duvet. Then he trotted across the floor and slid silently under their bedroom door, out into the passage.

Lottie slid out of bed and limped over to sit on the end of Ruby's bed, listening, her heart thudding. She could feel Sofie, far away in her own dark bedroom, curled up on her pink-spotted duvet, listening too.

He is bound to do it wrong, she told Lottie edgily. *You should not have let him. He will get himself hurt.*

I couldn't stop him, Lottie sighed. *He was so furious.* "Oh!" she squeaked.

From down the corridor, there had been a strange scuffling noise, and then a horrible yell, followed by another, and another, three or four people screaming and squealing.

Ruby dashed out, and Lottie clambered off Ruby's bed and hobbled out into the corridor. "Um – what is it? Is it a fire?" she murmured, rather lamely. Other people from their class were coming out of their rooms too, looking scared. Lottie limped along to where Zara's room was, just in time to see Zara fling open the door and run out, shoving Amy out of the way and flattening herself against the wall of the corridor. In the dim light from the one bulb hanging over the stairs, Lottie could see that she was very pale.

Amy stumbled out after her, holding her arm and looking upset. "You banged me into the door," she said to Zara, her voice tiny with shock.

"Shut up!" Zara snapped. "Where did it go?"

Inside their room, which was one of the larger ones for three people, Bethany was standing on her bed, somehow twisted up inside her duvet, and still screaming.

"What's the matter with her?" Lottie asked, actually feeling quite worried. Bethany sounded as though she was going to scream herself sick.

"There's a mouse in there," Amy sobbed. "Beth hates mice. Ow, my arm. . ."

"Aren't you going to help her?" Ruby asked Zara, and everyone in the corridor stared at Zara, waiting for her to run in and pull her best friend out.

She didn't. She looked down at her feet, and then up and down the corridor, as though she hoped Mrs Laurence would arrive and sort things out.

Lottie gave her a disgusted look and hobbled into the room, putting the light on. The sudden brightness stopped Bethany's screams, although she was still crying, and she gazed helplessly at Lottie, and Ruby hovering behind her.

"Come on. I'm sure the mouse has gone," Lottie told her gently, trying not to laugh. The mouse in question had run up her bare foot, and was currently clinging just inside her pyjama leg. He tickled.

Lottie pulled at Bethany's duvet, trying to untangle her, and Bethany clung on to her arm, shivering. Lottie almost felt guilty. How could anyone be that scared of a tiny little mouse? She tugged Bethany off the bed, and she and Ruby half-dragged, half-carried her out into the corridor.

"It was chewing my hair!" Zara was telling everyone else, as Lottie staggered out with Bethany. "It was awful!" But it wasn't having the effect she wanted. Everyone was looking at Bethany, tear-stained and shaking, and then back at Zara, who'd run out and left her.

"There's a spare bed in our room," Lily told Bethany. "Do you want to come and share with us?"

"Please. . . But Amy. . ." Bethany looked round for her. "Where's she going to sleep?"

Ruby darted back into their room and grabbed the duvets off two of the beds. "You can use them like a sleeping bag on the floor," she told Amy. "Is your arm OK now?"

Amy nodded, and everyone remembered how she'd been hurt, and stared at Zara again.

And then somehow, everyone melted away and left Zara alone, standing in the corridor outside her bedroom – where she'd have to spend the rest of the night with the invisible mouse.

Lottie stared out of the coach window, watching hungrily for something she recognized. They could only be about half an hour away now, she was sure. She could feel Sofie's voice growing stronger and stronger in her head. Sofie was wandering round the shop, her claws clicking on the boards in an impatient rhythm and driving Uncle Jack mad.

Soon, she promised.

Tell the driver to go faster, Sofie growled back. *Where is that girl?*

Up at the front. No one saved her a seat – I don't think that's ever happened to Zara before. Lottie peeked up over the seats in front and saw Zara, huddled in a seat on her own behind Mrs Laurence. She looked smaller, somehow. Fred spied out of her pocket and chuckled to himself.

Hmm. I may have to tell the mouse he is not entirely useless, Sofie muttered regretfully.

Oh, I just saw a sign for Netherbridge! Sofie, tell Mum and Dad you all need to come and get me, we're almost there!

"Ruby, look, we're nearly home!" Lottie nudged Ruby, who was half-asleep, and sat clutching the edge of the window, digging her fingernails in her palms, waiting.

All the parents were standing outside the school, and Lottie searched anxiously for hers.

I can see you! Get off that big – bus thing! Sofie yelled at her.

Lottie scrambled down the aisle, ignoring Mrs Laurence telling everyone to go slowly and be sensible, and was met by a small black furry bullet, speeding up the coach steps and into her arms.

Oh, I missed you! she half-cried to Sofie.

Never go away again!

I promise. Next time we'll make you invisible somehow and you can come too, I don't care how hard it is to do.

Her dad was pulling her gently down the steps so that everyone else could get out, and she could hear her mum apologizing to Mrs Laurence, but Lottie didn't care. The hole that had been inside her for the last five days had closed up, and now she was solid and real again.

"Do I get a hug anytime soon?" her dad asked, after he'd fetched Lottie's bag from the coach.

"Sorry!" Lottie gasped, and hugged him one-armed, and then her mum too. "Are you OK? Nothing's gone wrong in the shop?"

Her dad grinned. "No, we survived five days without you."

"Where is Ruby?" Sofie muttered in Lottie's ear, and Lottie giggled as Sofie's snuffly whiskers tickled her. "She's over there, why?"

"Take me to her," Sofie commanded, and Lottie carried her over, loving the feeling of Sofie's warm little body tucked in her arms again.

Ruby was telling her mum all about the trip. "Hey, Lottie. Does your uncle Jack want us to come and get Sam and Joe now?"

Lottie looked blank for a second, then smiled as Sofie crossly spat rude French insults inside her head. *Yes! Get rid of them, they are a menace! And so conceited. I have never heard so much nonsense about dragons.*

"I'm sure that would be OK." She leant closer to Ruby and whispered, "Sofie wants to talk to you."

Hand me to her.

Really? Lottie blinked. Sofie wasn't usually keen on being cuddled by anyone else.

Sofie scrambled into Ruby's arms and snuffled her cheek lovingly. "You are a good girl," she whispered, taking advantage of Ruby and Tara's mums discussing the amount of mud all over everyone. "A good girl, taking care of my Lottie. We will show you how grateful we are, you will see."

Ruby smiled at her in surprise. "I didn't really do much. . ." she whispered back.

Sofie only nodded solemnly. "You will see."

"Hi Ruby, did you have a good time?" Lottie's mum called. "Lottie, come on. You need to go and have a bath and soak off all this mud. Ruby can come over to the shop later to pick up Sam and Joe."

Sofie snorted in agreement. *I love you, Lottie,* she assured her, *but you smell.*

Chapter 9

There was only a week back at school after the trip, before the Christmas holidays. Lottie had been so worried about the idea of being without Sofie for a week that she'd hardly thought about Christmas, and she realized with horror that she had no presents for anyone. She especially wanted to get something gorgeous for Sofie, to show how much she had missed her, and for Ruby too, to say thank you for looking out for her so much while they were away. Plus she needed to buy something for her dad, which she'd never had to do before.

Luckily Mum promised to take her shopping in Foxley, a town a few miles away that had a lot more present-y sort of shops than Netherbridge. Lottie didn't want to give everybody soap or chocolates, and that was about all the Netherbridge shops could manage. Lottie was really looking forward to a day out, just her and her mum – although of course she wouldn't complain if her dad decided to come too.

"Are you going to give Danny a present?" Ruby muttered. She and Lottie had ended up in a well-placed position in assembly, right behind Tom Moffat, who was the tallest boy in the school. None of the teachers could see them whispering. "Oh, no, look! Mr Midgely's got a Christmas jumper on again. I think his mum knits them for him. It's actually got sequins on for the Christmas tree decorations."

"Well, Mrs Laurence's got light-up candy cane earrings. It's like they've all gone Christmas-mad." Lottie shrugged. "And I don't know about Danny."

"He didn't buy you a birthday present. Or even a card," Ruby pointed out.

Lottie nodded. "I know. I know he's being a

total pain. But he's so miserable, Ruby! He misses Sep like mad, now, as well. I'd never say it to Uncle Jack, but I don't think he should have stopped Danny taking Sep to school. Danny hates school, and Sep was the only thing making it OK for him. So now he hates being at home and school's even worse!" She sighed. "At least he can be at home with Sep now it's the holidays."

"Don't you dare start feeling guilty!" Ruby hissed at her.

Lottie looked up at her, surprised. "I don't!" She started pleating the edge of her Christmas carol sheet. "OK, maybe I do a teensy bit. It *is* my fault he's so unhappy."

"Uh-uh. Your dad's fault. Pandora's, maybe your mum's. You didn't make all this happen, did you?"

Lottie smiled to herself. She knew what Ruby meant, but actually, she had, a lot of it. Every so often, despite the horribleness of Danny, it struck her just how much she had done in the last few months. How the old Lottie, who didn't even remember Netherbridge, wouldn't believe what her life was like now. Even if her parents never got back together (and she wasn't giving up on that) at least they were *there*! She had a dad again. She could cope with Danny — although not if there were any more spiders.

She grinned. "I might buy him a furry toy tarantula. With a Santa hat. . . Hey, shhh, Mrs Laurence's looking at us."

Lottie got home from school, and unwound her new scarf gratefully as the warmth of the shop hit her. "That feels so good," she told Sofie happily. "It's absolutely freezing out there. I wouldn't be surprised if it snowed."

"Ugh." Sofie snorted and shivered.

"Don't you like snow?" Lottie asked. She loved it, and she'd hardly ever seen snow actually at Christmas. Somehow Netherbridge seemed like the sort of place that would have beautiful crisp white snow.

"Lottie, if you were more *petite* like me—" somehow Sofie managed to imply that Lottie was the size of an elephant in the way she said this "—then you would not like that cold wet stuff either."

Lottie tried not to laugh at the thought of Sofie half-swimming through a snowdrift with just her nose showing, but it wasn't much use, as Sofie could see what she was thinking.

Sofie flapped her ears irritably. "Hmf. So you see, if it snows, I shall be staying inside." She stalked back to her purple velvet cushion by the counter.

"Oh, Sofie, don't sulk! It's the beginning of the Christmas holidays. And I need your help thinking what presents to buy people."

Sofie sprang up immediately. "Shopping! Let us go and look on the computer." She trotted into the little office next to the kitchen and hopped up on to the computer chair. Lottie squeezed in beside her.

"Mmm. Your mother would look nice in a hat like that, Lottie. Click on it. No, that one! Really, Lottie! Would I ever suggest that colour for your mother? She would look like a strawberry, she has not the colouring. Now, I, of course, look very good in red." Sofie flicked her whiskers, preening happily, and Lottie hugged her.

"You really do." Lottie eyed Sofie thoughtfully. Would she like a little coat for Christmas? A red one?

"What?"

"Nothing! It isn't fair, Sofie. I want to get you a Christmas present, but I can't surprise you."

Sofie ducked her head shyly, and looked up at Lottie sideways, her eyes sparkling with excitement. "For me? I will not look, Lottie, I promise." She turned briskly back to the screen. "And what are we going to do about Daniel, hmm?"

Lottie sighed. "I don't know. Ruby thinks he

doesn't deserve a Christmas present, but that seems mean."

"Huh. *He* is mean, that one," Sofie muttered. "But you are right. We are very, very nice. He can have a small present."

"Where is he, anyway?" Lottie glanced at the clock in the corner of the screen. "He should be back by now, shouldn't he? He told Uncle Jack this morning that they were breaking up at one. The bus should have got back to Netherbridge ages ago." The secondary school that Danny went to was in the next town.

Sofie shrugged, her nose pressed up close to the computer. "He is probably just late, like always. Look, this is a pretty necklace, no?"

But Lottie wasn't looking.

"Lott-eee!" Sofie jumped on to her lap and stared up at her with troubled dark eyes. "What, you think there is something really wrong?"

Lottie shrugged. "I just can't help thinking

138

about that time he tried to show off to those boys in his class, and he ended up getting hurt. What if he's done something stupid?"

Sofie jumped gracefully down. "Let us go and interview that Septimus. He should know."

"He isn't there," Lottie said frustratedly, as they peered into Sep's cage.

"Pssst."

Lottie glanced over to see Fred on the next shelf, leaning over to whisper. "He's behind the cage."

"What? Why?" Lottie asked worriedly.

Fred shrugged. "Sulking. He won't say, but we think Danny's not talking to him."

Lottie's eyes widened, and she looked down anxiously at Sofie.

"Find him," Sofie snapped. "Get him out here." Her tail was straight down, almost tucked between her legs, which always meant something was wrong.

Lottie reached in and very gently edged the cage away from the wall. Behind it, Septimus was curled up in a little black ball. He looked even smaller than one of the mice.

Lottie stretched out her hand gingerly. Usually she would never be scared that one of the animals would bite her, but Sep wasn't himself. If Danny had torn away from him, it meant something was very wrong with both of them.

She stroked the furry ball gently, and felt a shiver run down Sep's spine. "Go away, Lottie," he murmured.

"Sep, I need to talk to you."

"I can't."

"You have to!" Sofie gave a sharp little bark, and the magic in it made Lottie's skin crawl. It uncoiled Sep from his stubborn ball, with his teeth bared and a desperate look in his eyes.

"Sep, listen. Where's Danny? Something's wrong, I'm sure of it. More than just that he's angry with you, I mean."

"He's at school," Sep muttered wearily,

starting to pad back into the dark quiet space behind his cage.

"No – no, he can't be. School's finished, Sep, it's the last day of term."

"He should have been home by now," Sofie yapped sharply.

Sep turned round, his whiskers twitching faintly. "He should be back?"

"*Exactement.*"

"He could just be walking slowly. . ." Sep murmured, but his eyes were darting around the shop, as though he hoped to find Danny lurking there somewhere. Then he closed them, clearly trying to reach Danny in his head. He was silent for a moment, stone-still – and then he sagged. "He's shut me out, but I can still reach just a little of him, if I search hard enough. He feels desperate, Lottie." Sep surged to the front of the shelf and jumped on to Lottie's shoulder. "Where can he have gone? We have to find him!"

"Can't you tell where he is?" Lottie asked,

peering down at Sep.

The rat hung his head, his whiskers drooping. "I don't know. He told me to go. He didn't want me any more. It's like I said, I only have a wisp of him now."

Lottie flinched – it was as though the words actually hurt her inside. "He's very. . ." She paused, trying to pin down the right word, and at last she shrugged a little and added, "He's angry, Sep. Mostly with me. He shouldn't have taken it out on you."

Sofie scrambled into Lottie's arms and put her nose to Sep's. "He is taking it out on you, Septimus, because he knows it is safe."

"Don't understand," Sep muttered dully.

"Idiot rat! Because he knows that whatever he does to you, you cannot stop loving him! Like I cannot stop loving Lottie!"

Sep's whiskers sprang out like they were on springs, and he stared at Sofie, glittery-eyed. "You think I can find him?"

"Ugh! *Imbécile!* Where – is – he? He cannot

break his ties with you so easily. Find him!"

Sep shook himself, his tail coiling from side to side as he stared into the distance. "The station."

"Should we tell Uncle Jack?" Lottie murmured, hearing her uncle pottering about in the storeroom. Her mum was singing along to the radio in the kitchen.

Sofie shook her ears determinedly. "I think not. Just us."

"OK. Mum! I'm just nipping out to see Ruby, all right? It's about homework." Lottie crossed her fingers. She didn't like lying to Mum, but it was for a good reason. She grabbed her coat and was out of the door before anyone had a chance to argue.

Lottie hadn't been to Netherbridge Station for ages. It was an old grey stone building with white-painted ironwork. It looked as though it ought to be full of steam trains, not diesel locomotives with automatic doors and sandwich trolleys. There was only one line with two tiny platforms, each only big enough for a bench.

The station was almost completely deserted – except that on the nearest bench was Danny.

"What are you doing here?" he snarled at her.

"I came to talk to you." Lottie sat down next to him, but not too close. She still remembered the spider.

"How did you know where I was?" Danny muttered. "Oh. Sep. Thought I told you to get lost."

It was at this point, seeing Sep's eyes close with pain, that Lottie lost her temper. "Don't you dare talk to him like that!" she yelled.

"Talk to him how I like, he's my rat," Danny growled, but his eyes had widened in surprise.

"Exactly," Lottie snapped. "He's yours. So you can start to look after him, instead of being so disgustingly selfish. Look at him." She grabbed Danny's hand and dumped Sep in it. "His fur's gone dull, he's so miserable."

"Am I really yours?" Sep asked, wrapping himself round Danny's fingers.

Danny heaved a great, shaky sigh, and ran a loving finger down Sep's back. "Yes," he admitted. "I should never have said you weren't, Sep, I'm sorry."

"Why did you?" Lottie asked. "I don't get it. When I had to go on that school trip without Sofie it was like torture. How could you do that to yourself? And him?"

"If I did it, then Dad couldn't," Danny muttered. He sighed. "Look. Dad made me behave before by putting a spell on Sep, right? So I thought, if I kept Sep as my familiar, Dad would always be able to make me do what he wanted. Like blackmail. I didn't want Dad bossing me around." He lifted Sep up on to his shoulder, stroking him lovingly, and Sep snuggled against his neck. "But I don't care. I can't go through with it. Dad can do what

145

he likes."

"I bet if you talked to your dad, he'd let Sep go back with you to school after Christmas," Lottie suggested.

Danny laughed. "I wasn't going back to school at all, Lottie. I've got all my money with me. I was running away."

"Was?" Lottie asked hopefully.

Danny shrugged. "It's a bit cold," he muttered.

"Very cold," Sep agreed. "We could use the money to go and buy some peanut brittle at the sweet shop instead. It's on the way home."

Danny stood up, stretching his knees and making a face, as though he'd been sitting on that bench for a very long time. "All right." He looked at Lottie, sideways and rather shy. "You want some?" he offered apologetically.

Lottie nodded. She had a feeling it was as close to *sorry* as she was going to get.

"Your turn, Fred." Lottie picked out a large

parcel and put it down in front of Fred. He couldn't possibly have held it – it was at least six times his size.

"All of it? For me?" Fred scampered round his parcel twice and leant against it lovingly.

"You are supposed to unwrap it," Sofie told him grumpily. She knew what it was, but she still wasn't happy that his parcel was larger than hers.

"Ohhh. . ." Fred had peeled off the paper and was now standing with both paws pressed against the box, feasting his eyes on the cellophane window that showed the contents. "Rainbow sugar. Oh, Lottie. It's perfect."

Sofie was leaning against Lottie's arm very hard, in a way that suggested it really ought to be her turn next. Lottie handed her a smartly wrapped parcel. "Mum and I found it online. I had to order it from France."

Sofie's ears twitched with excitement. "*Mais oui*," she muttered. "*Naturellement*. Ah!" She had nosed the parcel open at last, and pulled

147

out a little red fleece coat with a natty black braid.

"It's specially designed for a dachshund," Lottie told her anxiously. "To be long enough. Do you like it?"

"I do." Sofie allowed Lottie to put the coat on her, and twirled around, preening and admiring herself. "But this does not mean I am going out in that snow, Lottie. Or at least, I will not walk in it. Perhaps, if I have this on, you may carry me."

Lottie nodded, laughing. The snow had started to fall on Christmas Eve, and Sofie hadn't stirred from the house since. Of course, that was partly because she refused to leave the kitchen, where Lottie's mum and Uncle Jack had been arguing about exactly what had to be part of Christmas dinner. Uncle Jack was not a fan of sprouts, but Lottie's mum said they were traditional, and Lottie's dad was backing her up – even though Uncle Jack swore blind that he had never seen his brother eat a sprout in his life.

Sofie hadn't helped by stating flatly that Christmas pudding was disgusting, and English, and inedible, but at least they had stopped arguing while they told her how completely wrong she was.

Lottie grinned to herself as she watched Danny opening a present from her mum and dad – a computer game she'd told her mum he'd really like – and even managing to give her mum a polite hug to say thank you. She'd given him a huge jar of mint humbugs, which were his and Sep's favourite thing after peanut brittle.

She only had one present left to hand out, and she couldn't really wrap that one. Ruby had promised to come over for an hour before Christmas lunch at her parents' house, and Lottie had told her to bring Sam and Joe too.

Lottie picked up some of her huge pile of presents – even Danny had bought her a bracelet, and it was actually nice – and carried them upstairs. She needed to use the time before Ruby arrived to practise the spell again.

"Do you want me to take that off for you?" she asked Sofie, watching the little dog panting in the scarlet coat as she bounced up the stairs.

"No!" Sofie shook her head, and simply bounced a little higher, so that she was almost floating up the stairs instead.

Delicious smells of turkey were floating up the stairs and making Sofie drool delicately by the time Ruby put her head round the bedroom.

"Happy Christmas! Your mum said you were up here. Are you OK?"

Lottie nodded. "Definitely. I've got your present up here, that's all."

Sam and Joe eased themselves out of Ruby's rucksack slowly.

"Hello, Lottie," Sam growled. "This weather's murder. I feel like my blood's gone to treacle."

"Good smell, though," Joe pointed out,

sniffing turkey from downstairs.

"This is your present." Lottie glanced at Sofie, and Fred, who was helping too, even though he refused to come out of the sleeve of her cardigan – the lizards upset him.

"What is?" Ruby glanced around, looking confused.

"You have to sit down. And hold Sam and Joe." Lottie sat down on the floor and gestured to Ruby to sit opposite her. "There's good." She pulled the big black-bound book she'd borrowed from Ariadne towards her and ran her finger down the words. "OK. I really hope you like this, because I don't think I can undo it again." With Sofie pressed close against her, and making a strange low humming growl in her throat, Lottie started to speak the spell, reaching out to tap her fingers against Sam and Joe's scales. She scattered a pinch of glittery dust over them, dust that she'd made herself from feathers she'd found on Netherbridge Hill. She'd added a strange little scrap of coarse silvery hair that she'd pulled from a bramble bush, just where the unicorns had thundered down the hill on her birthday.

At last she sat back, sighing wearily, and staring at the lizards. Sofie stared too, and Ruby frowned at them both.

"What *was* that?" she whispered.

"Look!" Lottie's voice squeaked with excitement, and she pointed at Sam, who was wriggling and stretching and looking confused. Joe was starting to twist and shake his head.

"Something odd. . ." Sam gasped.

"Very odd!" Joe muttered. "Hey!" He gave a sudden little jerk, as though he had hiccups, and a pair of beautiful, parchment-thin wings suddenly shot out of his back.

Seconds later, Sam stretched out his own wings, silver-blue and practically transparent, spread between tough darker blue ribs, like a bat's.

"You gave them wings!" Ruby breathed,

gazing down at them in delight.

Lottie shook her head. "No. They always said they ought to have them – I only found the wings for them, that's all."

"You knew we were dragons really, didn't you, Ruby dearest?" Sam asked her fondly.

Ruby shook her head. "I sort of hoped. . ." she whispered. "Lottie, thank you!"

Joe gave a hopeful sort of cough, and sighed. "No fire, then?" he asked Lottie sadly.

"I'm not good enough at magic for that yet," Lottie said apologetically.

Sofie nudged her lovingly. "But you will be, Lottie mine." Then she scowled at Joe. "Which is not to say that she would waste it on turning you into a fire hazard. She has much better things to do."

Lottie smiled, watching Sam flapping experimentally, and managing to get half of himself airborne.

Fred gave a horrified squeak as Sam flapped his wings again, this time launching himself across the room and gliding down on to Lottie's bed. Then he half-wriggled out of Lottie's sleeve and looked up hopefully. "Could you make wings for me, Lottie?"

Sofie shook her head vigorously, her ears flapping. "Over my dead body. I am not having flying mice in my shop."

Lottie hugged her, smiling. She hoped Sofie was right, and the magic would just keep on growing. Spells felt even better than sharing chocolate with Sofie and Ruby and Fred. Who knew what would happen next? Magic sparkled inside her, as she leaned her cheek on Sofie's velvet fur.

Although Sofie drinks enormous amounts of coffee and gobbles chocolate, this is only because she is a magical dog. Chocolate can be very dangerous for dogs, so please don't feed your dogs chocolate, or anything that isn't their normal food. Even if you suspect they're magical inside!

–HW

Enter the magical world of

the ordinary girl in an
extraordinary family...

HOLLY WEBB

EMILY FEATHER

and the Enchanted Door

1

Emily leaned over her mum's shoulder, hugging her carefully so as not to dribble the open tin of golden syrup that Emily was about to put in her flapjack mixture. "I like that one," she said thoughtfully, pointing at the fabric sample her mum was holding out, a soft strip of blue scattered with flowers and tiny birds.

"Not the red?" Her mum wafted it at her enticingly, so that the fierce bright-orange butterflies fluttered over the fabric. The red silk glittered, only a shade brighter than her mum's hair.

Emily blinked. For a second it had looked like one of the butterflies had lifted out of the fabric and floated idly across the kitchen to the window. She wrinkled her nose and squeezed her eyelids shut for a second. It was the bright sunshine getting in her eyes. "No, I really like the blue one. It's prettier. Is it for a dress? Is this a new collection for the shop?"

"Yes, we're thinking about next summer's clothes already. I think it's going to be a skirt, this one," her mum said thoughtfully. "A maxi-skirt, with jewels scattered through the flowers. They'll have to be hand-sewn; it'll be expensive." She padded out of the kitchen, trailing wings of soft, sheer fabric behind her, so that she looked like a butterfly too.

Emily giggled. When her mum was designing clothes, she sometimes forgot about everything else. Even meals. But then, she did make the most beautiful things, and not just for the shop; she made them for Emily and her sisters too. So it made up for having to make their own lunch, and dinner, a lot of the time.

For Emily's last birthday, her mum had made her a hat that looked like a cupcake, with pink icing and little sugar flowers on it. The kind of cake that Emily really loved making. The hat was one of her favourite things, and she wore it loads. It was much too hot for hats now, though. Emily leaned out of the window to breathe a bit. It was roasting in the kitchen, with the oven on. Still, it would be worth it. Flapjacks were one of her best recipes. She loved the way you just had to melt the buttery gooey mess together and stir a bit, and then it magically turned into cakey stuff when you cooked it.

"Emily!" Lark was yelling at her from down the garden. "Ems! Are you coming out? You'll melt if you stay inside all day!"

"I'm coming in a minute," Emily called back. "I just want to put these flapjacks in."

"It's too hot for cooking! You're mad! Honestly, Ems, I worry about you sometimes!" Lory joined in. "Come and sunbathe."

"I'm nearly done," Emily shouted out of the window. "And it won't stop you eating them, anyway, will it?"

She scooped the mixture into the tin, and then made a face at the washing up. She'd pile it into the sink and leave it till later. No one would mind. Her mum looked like she was going to be shut up in her studio for hours anyway, and her dad was in the tiny room under the stairs where he wrote his books. He wrote scary fantasy novels, and he was quite famous. He used his full name for the books, though – Ashcroft Feather, instead of just Ash, which was what most people called him. He hadn't even bothered coming out for lunch. He was stuck, he'd told everybody grumpily at breakfast, and he'd made Emily suggest ideas for really scary monsters while she was trying to eat her toast. It had slightly put her off her jam.

Emily peered out of the window at the blazing sun and decided to tie her hair back. It was too hot hanging round her neck. She wandered over to the wooden dresser that took up one wall of the kitchen. There was a mug full of hairbands and bits of ribbon on there somewhere, she was sure. It was while she was picking out a band that she found the photo, tucked under one of Lark and Lory's magazines. Emily pulled it out and stood it up on a shelf. She loved this photo. It was a rare one of all the children, sitting on the big old sofa in the living room. It had been taken when Robin was little – just turning from a baby into a boy, and losing his round, chubby face and the wispy, fair baby curls. His hair was darkening to red, and that pointed chin was starting to show. It was an odd photo, not much like other people's family portraits. Lark and Lory looked serious, and Robin was staring wide-eyed at the camera. Only Emily was smiling, in the middle of Lark and Lory, a dark-eyed, dark-haired, golden-tanned five-year-old, with Robin clutched on her lap.

The photo was in a little seashell frame, and it always lived on the dresser. But most of the time it was hard to see, because there was so much other stuff on there too. Fabric samples, and a scattering of beads. Homework. The dog's comb. Sheets of manuscript from their dad's latest novel, covered in scribble, and possibly torn into pieces. Vases of drooping flowers that Lark and Lory had brought in from the garden. But just occasionally, when it was tidy – which was usually only when her mum was lost for inspiration, and drifting around looking for something to do – the picture could be seen.

"Why does Robin look like Lark and Lory, and not like me?" Emily had asked her mum once, picking up the frame and running her fingers over the dusty shells.

Her mother had stopped on her way through to her studio, and stared at Emily for a second, her grey-blue eyes wide, before she smiled. "It just happens that way sometimes, Emily, flower. You got your looks passed on from another relative, I should think. It's just like Lory's yellow hair," she added. "No one else in the family has hair like that. We're all different."

Except that, actually, they weren't. Lory had yellow hair, it was true, but her features were just like their dad's. Her mum and dad actually looked quite alike too, Emily realized, sweeping a golden syrup drip off the side of the tin with her finger and sucking it as she went out into the garden. It was only her. She wished she knew whichever relative it was that she looked like.

Emily's house had a strange garden – it was the same size as all the other gardens on the street, but it seemed bigger somehow, and more private, because it was surrounded by trees. It was a useless sort of garden for football, or anything that needed a lawn, because there wasn't one – but it was full of tunnels, and holes, and twisted old trees, and it was perfect for playing hide-and-seek. Lark and Lory were out there somewhere, but as Emily let herself out by the back door and stood hesitating on the step, she couldn't see them at all. She could hear them, though: sharp, sweet giggling, and then a muttered comment and a riffle of pages, and another burst of laughter.

"Lark! Lory!" She set off down one of the little brick paths, calling for them. The sun was blinding, and she held her arm up across her eyes, pulling her hot hair back into the band and making for the shade under a clump of thorn trees at the edge of the garden. Where were Lark and Lory hiding?

Suddenly, Lark and Lory's voices came to her, as clear as little ringing bells, or the sharp twittering of the birds gathered above her in the thorn tree.

Emily stumbled on up the path. The sun was so bright that she was half-blinded, and she blinked as the light flickered, filtering down through the trees above her in dark bars of shadow and sunlight.

"Emily, what are you doing?" one of her sisters giggled. A thin-fingered hand caught hers and pulled her down on to a rug laid over the mossy grass. Gruff, their huge black dog, opened one eye to see who'd turned up, grunted, and went back to sleep again.

"You looked like you were about to fall over," Lark

said, wrapping an arm round her shoulders and staring worriedly into her eyes. "Are you OK? You look wobbly."

"I'm fine." Emily stretched out on the rug next to her and peered at their magazine. "I guess you were right; I was melting indoors. It's much nicer out here."

"You could have brought us a drink, Ems," Lory complained.

Emily rolled her eyes but didn't say anything. Lory was so bossy sometimes. Lark was a bit more easygoing, but now that her sisters had turned thirteen, they seemed an awful lot older than they had only a few weeks ago. Too old to hang around with their little ten-year-old sister, a lot of the time.

Arguing with Lory and Lark was pointless. They always worked as a double act, and it was impossible to get the better of them. They were both staring at her now, and smiling, their heads together. The same smile, even though they weren't identical twins, and didn't, at first glance, look that much alike. Lark's streaky brown hair was nothing like Lory's golden blonde, and their eyes were different too; Lark's were much darker. But now they couldn't be anything but sisters.

Emily twirled a strand of her own dark curly hair around one finger and peered down at the magazine. The girl in the photo had dark hair like hers, with a pretty scarf tied round it. She'd like something like that.

"Are you going shopping in town later?" she asked Lark hopefully. "Can I come too?"

Lark and Lory looked at each other thoughtfully, and then Lark said, "Maybe. . ."

"She means no," someone called from above their heads, and all three girls yelped in surprise. Lory threw the magazine at the red-haired boy leaning out of the tree above them.

"Were you spying on us?"

"Only a little bit," Robin said, laughing. He flipped round so that he was hanging off the branch by his knees, and Emily shuddered.

"Don't do that! You'll fall!"

"No, I won't. . ." Robin pushed against the tree trunk, so he was swinging. "I never fall," he added smugly. "Unless I want to." He swung his hands back up again, to grab one of the thinner branches, and then dangled himself down, kicking at Lory's magazine, which was stuck halfway up the trunk. "There! Got it!" It fluttered to the ground, and Robin dropped after it, landing sprawled across Lark and Lory's knees, and giggling as though it was the funniest thing he'd ever seen.

Emily stared down at him. She didn't look a bit like Robin either. He had blazing red hair like Eva, their mother, and light blue-grey eyes, and the same sharp chin and pale colouring as Lark and Lory. As he lay there giggling and wriggling away from Lark, who was tickling him, Emily could see his perfect white teeth.

She curled her knees up, wrapping her arms around them, half-watching her sisters teasing him. Then something landed in her hair, and she squealed, and Robin rolled away, hooting with laughter. "Serves you right for daydreaming!" he spluttered.

"What is it? What is it?" Emily shook her ponytail frantically, batting at it with her hands. "Did you drop a spider on me? I'm going to strangle you, Robin Feather!"

"It's only a caterpillar. . ." Lark said soothingly,

picking something out of Emily's curls. She knew how much Emily hated spiders.

"No, it isn't." Robin rolled his eyes. "She's so scared of crawly things, I wouldn't even drop a caterpillar on her. It's just a catkin."

"So it is," Lark agreed. "See, Emily? Nothing to be scared of."

Emily growled, still running her fingers through her hair, just in case. But she felt better, a bit now that Robin had teased her. It was such a little brother thing to do. She was just being silly.

Of course she belonged.

Holly has always loved animals. As a child, she had two dogs, a cat, and at one point, nine gerbils (an accident). Holly's other love is books. Holly now lives in Reading with her husband, three sons and a very spoilt cat.